Also by Elizabeth Fritz

Surprise! Surprise!

Cousin Delia's Legacy

Hope's Journey

Trio

Assisted Living—or Dying?

Athena

Hunting Giovane

For Mary Lou

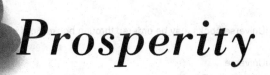

Prosperity

Elizabeth Fritz

iUniverse, Inc.
Bloomington

Prosperity

iUniverse books may be ordered through booksellers or by contacting:

iUniverse
1663 Liberty Drive
Bloomington, IN 47403
www.iuniverse.com
1-800-Authors (1-800-288-4677)

ISBN: 978-1-4620-1981-6 (sc)
ISBN: 978-1-4620-2378-3 (e)

Printed in the United States of America

iUniverse rev. date: 05/20/2011

AN EXPLANATION

Having been named Katharine Culhane's literary executor,* I was sorting through her unpublished manuscripts when I encountered this rather interesting autobiographical insight into my friend's life. I thought it worthy of sharing it with her reading public.

—Elizabeth Fritz

---

*Disclaimer: Katharine Culhane is a fictional character who has lived a fictional life and was a fictional friend of Elizabeth Fritz.

❧ 1 ❧

It was the Friday before Labor Day, 1950, that I stepped off the bus in Prosperity, Indiana. The sum total of my possessions resided in two battered suitcases. My future resided in a letter from Mr. Solomon Baumer bidding me to show myself on Tuesday after Labor Day to take up a position on his newspaper. My immediate past consisted of $98.00 in my purse and a diploma in one of the suitcases which attested to a bachelor's degree *magna cum laude* from Franklin College as of June 3, 1950. I had sent transcripts to a lot of newspapers, listing liberal arts courses with a major in journalism, including a letter of recommendation from my major professor, and had waited prayerfully for a reply. I received Mr. Baumer's reply gratefully—I was subsisting in the meantime on thirty-five cents an hour earned on the line of the Coca-Cola bottling plant in Fort Wayne while paying five dollars a week board and room to my father's Cousin Belle. I was growing desperate for a job. Ten weeks of inquiries had generated a discouraging collection of "no positions available" answers. Cousin Belle begrudged me every inch of space and every nibble of food and as soon as I conveyed the content of Mr. Baumer's letter, she couldn't wait to see me go. She didn't even tell me to write and say how

I was getting along. That was OK with me, I didn't care much for her either.

Now I stood on the sidewalk in front of the general store that served also as the bus station, breathing the hot, dusty air of that August afternoon and wondering what to do next. I looked up and down the wide, empty street in which none of the diagonal parking places was occupied, and at the fifteen or twenty store fronts that lined the street before it became a tree-shaded thoroughfare of modest houses. Off to the left I saw a sign that said "Radio Crier." Since that matched the letterhead of Mr. Baumer's missive, I picked up my suitcases and headed in its direction. As I stumbled along, I made mental notes of Prosperity's casual approach to street maintenance. Now that I was about to be a reporter, frost-heaved sidewalk slabs and potholed paving had potential for future news items. All the stores along my way were shut up tight, CLOSED signs propped inside the glass.

Arriving beneath *The Crier*'s sign, I pushed aside a torn screen door and tried the inner door. It opened to the tune of a jangling bell. Interior décor was less than prepossessing: a linoleum floor worn down to its backing; a window remarkable for the size and number of its smudges; and spider webs of prize-winning proportions draped over sagging mini-blinds. A long counter divided the space into two sections, the front furnished with half a dozen beat-up armless chairs, the back partially closed off by an eight-foot partition of batten board. I barged inside with my clumsy burden of luggage and took deep breaths of the unexpected blessing of cool air. A job in an air-conditioned enterprise was more than I had hoped for.

A teenager, face and hands ink-smudged, wearing a paper

hat, and wiping his hands on an inky rag, came from the back in response to the summons of the bell. Norman Rockwell would have found him prime material for a *Saturday Evening Post* cover but his vernacular was pure Hoosier.

"Ain't no one here but me. Everybody's gone to the Fair. If you want to place an ad, you'll have to come back tomorrow morning early before Mr. B and Sally goes to the Fair again." (The Fair, I thought, must be a major event around here. I was to hear its capital letter every time anyone spoke of it.)

"My name's Culhane. I'm supposed to go to work here next Tuesday."

"Oh yeah, Mr. B said you was on the way. But he didn't leave no word what I was supposed to do with you if you come when he was gone. Hard to tell when he'll be back today; they got flat racing goin' at the grounds and he likes to see it through."

The kid cocked his head on one side and looked mildly interested in what would happen next; apparently he felt once he had the ball back in my court, his work was done. Well, I wasn't going to let him think I was some hick without a clue, so I adopted my most businesslike tone in reply.

"I'll need to find a place to stay. Can you direct me to a hotel?"

"Ain't no hotel. Mrs. Pace down the street boards folks. Maybe she's got something but she's prob'ly at the Fair too. You could sit on her front porch till she got back, it's shady over there. Big white house with a naked lady in a fountain in the front yard."

He jerked his thumb to the left to indicate the way to Mrs. Pace's establishment. I picked up my baggage and proceeded in that direction over more cock-eyed sidewalk slabs. My suitcases got heavier, the air got hotter and dustier with every step. I reached Mrs. Pace's shady front yard with a groan of relief. The smoothly cut lawn and tall trees promised a cool breeze; the promise did not materialize. With my whole heart I envied the naked lady standing under the stream of water pouring from the urn poised over her head. To stave off the threat of heat prostration I splashed some of her water on my face and dried it with an already grubby handkerchief. I climbed up a flight of eight steps to the shade of the porch, knocked on a screen door (the house door stood open) without an answer, and decided to sit and wait on one of Mrs. Pace's inviting white rocking chairs. Weariness, heat, and the rhythmic motion of the chair were soporific and I promptly fell fast asleep.

❧ 2 ❧

A hearty voice jogged me abruptly awake, "And who might you be?"

A large woman stood at the foot of the stairs. She was dressed in a brightly flowered cotton dress that strained across her very generous bosom and equally generous hips. A broad-brimmed straw hat crowned a pink face and brilliant blue eyes peering out of plump cheeks. The woman was carrying a basket on her arm, its contents covered with a red-checked napkin. As I struggled to rise from my chair to answer her question, she started to climb the stairs, puffing and panting, her face growing ever more pink. My alarm at her breathlessness was superseded by the need to explain my presence. Hastily I introduced myself.

"I'm Katharine Culhane. I'm going to work for Mr. Baumer starting Tuesday, but I need a place to stay until I can settle. The boy at the paper said you had rooms...."

"No, I ain't," she interrupted in a firm tone. "I'm all full up with folks likely to stay."

"Perhaps you could recommend another place?"

"Ain't no other place. You hungry?"

I tried to sound like I wasn't. "No, ma'am. I'm not."

"Well, have a cinnamon bun anyway. That snooty Miz Prouty

5

elbowed me out of a blue ribbon at the Fair today. And I made up my mind I wasn't leaving my entry there for them judges to scarf down behind the curtains. Here, have one!"

She pulled aside the red-checked napkin and held the basket out to me. I took a bun and bit it into it, expecting an ordinarily tasty bit of pastry. But, wow, it was gooood! Plump raisins and buttery cinnamon goo in the swirl, creamy vanilla icing somewhat damaged by the heat of the day. With my mouth full, I mumbled my thanks and swallowed.

Able again to speak, I said, "If the judges chose Miz Prouty's buns over yours, they were either related to her or she's a bake-off champion. This is delicious!"

"Glad to hear you like it. Have another one. I'm goin' in the house and make some phone calls to see if we can get you a place."

I sat down in the rocking chair, bun in either hand, and rocked and savored until my hands were empty. Then I used the naked lady's basin and my grubby handkerchief to clean up. Mrs. Pace returned, minus her basket.

"I didn't tell you but my name is Ma-Ry-a Pace. If you put it in the paper some time be sure to spell it right, M-A-R-I-A-H. Now, pick up them bags and come on through the house. I got you a room with Madam Anna. Her house is back there behind mine. She'll take you on for a week and if you suit, longer if you want."

Talking all the way, she took me into the house, down a dim, cool hall, out the back door, and down the garden path to a back gate.

"I can give you meals, breakfast and supper seven days a week, $3.00 a week; Madam Anna will give you a room for

$3.00 a week. It's so close, even in the winter it won't be no problem to go back and forth. This here is Madam Anna's side gate."

The gate in the tall board fence was latched with a dilapidated metal thing that threatened to fall off when touched. But Mrs. Pace dealt with it firmly and ushered me in through a yard that was a riot of flowering shrubs and beds. Huge trees shaded part of the yard; brilliant spreads of white, red, and pink impatiens glowed under them. A bank of black-eyed Susans swept across emerald green grass off to my right, and colorful pots planted with green stuff (herbs maybe?) and red or pink or white geraniums lined up along a grassy path to the back door of a house almost lost under a mammoth wisteria vine. Brushing aside a heavy purple plume of flowers dangling over some shallow steps, Mrs. Pace called out, "Here she is, Madam Anna. She'll have supper with me at six."

↝ 3 ↜

She bustled off leaving me confronting my new landlady as we stood in the gloom under the wisteria vine. Madam Anna was tall, maybe six feet, with the smooth oval face of an iconic Madonna, black brows, heavy black braids wound in a coronet, and startling grey eyes. She wore a washed-off blue denim farmer's shirt and a full skirt of some coarse dark cloth down to her ankles, men's shoes peeping from under the hem. When she spoke, her voice had a vaguely foreign flavor although her diction and grammar were both elegant and refined. She waved to me to come in but did not extend her hand to greet me until we were inside. The hand she extended to me then was a surprise, work-roughened, marked by ground-in grime, dirt-caked under and around beautifully shaped albeit short nails.

"My name is Katharine …" I began.

"Yes, Mariah told me. I am called Madam Anna here but my full name is Anna Petrovna Suvorov. Welcome to my house. I hope we will suit one another. Come this way, please."

She turned and led me down a hall past a glimpse of a spotlessly clean kitchen, past closed doors on either side of the hall, to a stair rising to the second floor. Upstairs she indicated an open bathroom door with a wave of her hand as she led me into a large front-corner bedroom. The room was light and airy, cool despite the August heat out of doors. Airiness was emphasized by the scantiness of furniture which consisted of a plain four-drawer bureau, a single bed with a pillow and white coverlet, a straight chair and a deal table, disposed with military precision on a brilliantly polished bare hardwood floor. Only plain white blinds dressed the windows. She opened a door to disclose a roomy closet and stood back, apparently awaiting my reaction.

"Yes, I think this will do quite well. Shall I pay you a week's rent today?"

"If you like." She turned and left the room to return with a floor lamp which she installed next to the bed.

"You will perhaps want to read. You will kindly excuse me if I do not know exactly how to attend to your needs. I am unaccustomed to having a lodger. Please ask for whatever will make you comfortable. I caution you against excessive use of hot water; the heater in the basement has a rather low capacity. You may use the washing apparatus in the basement for your laundry."

She turned and left the room. I noticed she held herself very erect, and only now could I try to assess her age. I guessed 60 plus, although not a thread of gray showed in the heavy crown of her hair. I learned much later that she was actually nearly 80 and her stiffly upright posture was due to a restrictive brace worn from hip to shoulder. I set my suitcases on top of one another along the wall, took out my bag of toiletries, and freshened up for supper. I left for Mrs. Pace's house at quarter to six. I saw no sign of Madam Anna as I went downstairs and through the house and yard. I must have lacked Mrs. Pace's masterly way with the gate latch because it fell off in my hand

and I saw no way to replace it. I laid it carefully on a brick next to the path with an intention to confess my vandalism upon my return.

I knocked on Mrs. Pace's back screen and hearing no reply, entered and followed my nose to a dining room where a big table set with six places and chairs took up the center of the room. A long sideboard stood on one wall; a shiny steel 12- or 15- cup coffee pot sat on one end, flanked by a sugar bowl and cream pitcher. As I entered from the hall, a skinny teen-ager bearing a large platter of meatloaf, potatoes, and carrots entered from the kitchen.

"Name's Harold, Miss Culhane. You're supposed to sit here," he said, pointing to a chair at the left at what I presumed was the foot of the table. "The others all got regular places."

He put his platter down and disappeared to the kitchen, appearing again with a bowl in each hand—green beans and pickled red beets. Then Mrs. Pace came in, her face no longer pink, now fuchsia, carrying a basket of freshly baked rolls. As she inspected the table, she rang a cow bell vigorously. The bell brought out "the others," two men and a woman. They took up positions each behind a chair and waited expectantly.

Mrs. Pace took her seat at the head of the table and announced, "Sit down and start eatin' while it's hot. We can do the introductions while we eat."

The company followed her order obediently and for a few minutes the only sounds to be heard were those of serving utensils clicking against china as the dishes were passed and plates were loaded from them.

"Miss Culhane, in this house we say grace but not until after the second helpings and we're ready for dessert. So tuck in.

I'll tell you who's who. This kid here is my son Harold, 12 years old and not good for much, although he's a fine student in his first year of high school. The lady is Miss Edith Winer, town librarian, and this big fella is Curtis Dillon, he does somethin' on the pipeline; this older fella is Barney Confert, he's a boss of the pipeline crew. Miss Edith has lived here for near ten years and Curt and Barney came a few months ago and likely to stay for another six months. Folks, this girl is Katharine Culhane, she's goin' to work for Sol over at *The Crier*, startin' Tuesday."

She accomplished all these introductions between hasty bites of potato. I nodded to each of my commensals and then took a few bites myself while sneaking glimpses at the others. The food was wonderful and everyone was so busy putting it away that I could look them over unnoticed. Harold was a nice-looking kid with an unruly mop of hair and a pleasant expression. He was tall for his age and his complexion was blessedly free of zits; he had his mother's blue eyes. Miss Edith was elderly, wispy, and garrulous; she could hardly wait to get a conversation going. Yes, she kept the library, open 9 to 5 Tuesday to Saturday, quite a nice collection of old and new books, all the classics; since I must be a college graduate I'd surely be interested in visiting. Then Barney, having demolished his first helpings of main course staples, decided it was time he took charge of the conversation and began questions. "Where you from? Got a boyfriend? Mariah says you're gonna sleep at Madam Anna's. Think you're gonna like it over there? She's not your usual kind of folks. But she does have a way with plants. Where was it you went to school? Franklin, eh? Can't be very proud of the sports record of that college. They haven't won a championship in 30 years of playing football. Now Curt here, he's a Purdue man, played varsity, graduated last year, civil engineering."

Curt blushed fiery red and ducked his head. He was putting away the victuals with single-minded attention; you could tell he knew what a dinner table was for. I'd not hear from him until after the food was gone and the plates polished clean. Barney was quite a trencherman; his build testified to that, belly bulging over his belt, pants tight over his thighs, shirt sleeves also tight around his arms. He was balding, weather-beaten, with a guardsman's mustache and bushy eyebrows. Curt was a blond, blue-eyed All-American boy, tall, broad-shouldered, slim-hipped, with an engaging though infrequent smile. His sunburn had yet to convert to tan. He spoke seldom but his smiles and nods were friendly.

Harold was sent to the kitchen for an enormous bowl of tapioca pudding and a cherry pie while each of us stacked our plates and silver ("Keep your fork" I was admonished) for Mariah to pick up and carry out. Grace was brief but fervent. Harold passed dessert plates and bowls and we immediately began to appreciate our pudding and pie. Harold served our coffee and made a trip to the kitchen for his glass of milk. I volunteered to help wash dishes but Mariah pursed her lips, and flicked a glance at Miss Edith who was saying, "Oh, no, you don't. That's my job." I wondered if Miss Edith might not get a reduction in her board for helping in the kitchen.

Mariah invited me to go to the parlor for conversation but I pled weariness and the need to unpack. But before I left for Madam Anna's house Mariah had me sign a dog-eared record of lodgers who had enjoyed her rooms and food over the past ten years. Proudly she emphasized the callings of some illustrious signatures. One overnight guest on the campaign trail went on to become a two-time governor of the state. "Remembered me every Christmas with a handwritten card. I've got 'em all saved in an album. I'll show you sometime." Tired as I was I tucked away the fact before I made my escape. My store of grist for future news items was adding up.

Walking through the Pace back yard, half of it a neat outlay of late season vegetables, half neatly trimmed grass, I reveled in the wondrous peace of the looming twilight and sweet smell of some flowering shrub. Then entering Madam Anna's yard and experiencing her glorious display pulled out all the stops of esthetic emotion. But I didn't linger and went into the house and up to my room without seeing or hearing anything of my hostess. I was thinking I would like Prosperity, if indications so far were omens of the future.

❧ 4 ❧

I wrote in my journal until my hand cramped and my eyes grew heavy.* Today had been a milestone in a life so far generally bland. When I was growing up, my dad was in the Pacific as a combat photographer; he now lived in Europe doing something for CARE. My mom had worked for the War Department in Washington, reading maps and collating aerial photographs, but she divorced Dad when I was ten and sent me to live with my maternal grandparents in Kansas. She was now married contentedly to a career Army officer moving from station to station on the post-war scene. Neither of my parents had ever figured more than marginally in my life, but I got along fine with my grandparents on the farm until they were killed in a car crash three years ago. Lucky in rural schooling with outstanding teachers, I had had no trouble qualifying for scholarships at Franklin. I made a few friends (actually no more than acquaintances) that I probably would not keep up with; I

---

*If ever this memoir meets a reader and he or she should wonder at my detailed recall of a day 50 years and more ago, let me remind him or her that my college education was in journalism and I expected to make a career in journalism. So I kept a journal and wrote it up nightly before bed. Upon review, I find my style rather florid but I was after all a neophyte at the writing business. Future contents are pretty ho-hum on the average but today must have seemed a special concatenation of people and events and the entry was long and detailed.

wasn't conditioned by my past for close or lasting relationships. Now, I was on the threshold of a career, ready to be optimistic about my future. I put down my pen, closed my journal, and crept into bed. My travel clock read 10:15.

The next morning I attended Mrs. Pace's bounteous breakfast buffet (hours 5:30-7) for bacon and eggs, oatmeal and toast, and coffee or tea. At 6, the pipeline guys had been and gone, Miss Edith hadn't yet risen, and Harold was already mowing the front yard. Mrs. Pace was preparing to return to the Fair. Today was crafts and ladies' handiwork day, and she had entered a log cabin quilt and a pair of pillow cases edged with tatted lace. She invited me along, but when I said I wanted to drop in at the paper first, she gave me directions to the fairground and told me not to let Sol Baumer put me to work early.

"He's a nice guy," she said, "but he's a Jew and bound to get something for nothing every chance he gets."

I found Mr. Baumer in his office behind the batten board partition. He was getting Sally Frye off to an early start on a day at the Fair. She was a younger but less garrulous version of Miss Edith Winer. Frizzy hair straggled out from under a baseball cap and her safari jacket sported cameras and accessories bulging from an array of pockets. After a perfunctory greeting, she hurried off, no time for chit chat. I took time to measure up Mr. Baumer whose first words were "Call me Sol!" Both face and body fitted the adjective "rotund." A skullcap (yarmulke?) perched precariously on his untidy grey coiffure. A wrinkled tie recapitulating the menus of recent and not so recent meals hung loose from an equally wrinkled shirt collar. A vintage typewriter teetered on the corner of his desk, almost edged off by piles of newspapers both whole and ragged from clipping. I noticed they were big city papers with non-current dates. Clearly, "untidy" was the adjective for both him and his milieu. But his brown eyes sparkled with intelligence and his smile was warm and friendly. He spoke in bullets. I answered in like form. His style was catching.

Where you from? Kansas! Why were you in Fort Wayne? Ever worked on a paper? No? Culhane, Irish name, you Catholic? No? Learn local churches—Saint Pius 10 miles away in Columbia, Wesley Chapel in downtown Prosperity, Redeemer Lutheran a mile south of town, First Baptist north edge of town—lots of news to be got from churches. Got a car? (I managed to get two words in here, "No, sir!") See Buzz at the implement store, rent a bicycle, you'll need one. What you doing today? No plans? Go to the Fair, pick up human interest stuff. Live by my rules: I give assignments, you report. You got something I didn't assign, pass it by me before you write it up. You can use that desk and typewriter over there. Turn up here every day by 8. Not Saturday, that's when I go to Columbia for shool. Paper goes to bed sundown Thursday, this is a weekly, you know. Deadline Thursday 11 P.M. Copy leaves then for the press in Columbia, print is back Friday noon. Got any questions?

"What's the pay?" I managed to get the words out despite my bewilderment.

"Twenty-five a week, make sure you earn it! If that's all, I'm leaving for the day."

"Yes sir, thank you, sir."

Settling his skullcap more firmly on his head, he bustled out the door and was gone. What's "shool" I wondered.

Rummaging the dictionary resting on a shelf above the desk provided the information that the word was really "shul" and meant synagogue. That meant Saturday was Sabbath for Sol and that I had learned something new. Sol was the first Jew I had ever known; Mrs. Pace had sounded like a bigot. Later, I learned she just took Jewishness for granted, stereotypes and all, no judgments attached.

I decided to explore the town before going to the Fair. There was not much town to explore and very few stores or shops were open. Hastert's Grocery was open but the sign on the door said, "CLOSING AT 10 FOR THE FAIR, OPEN AGAIN ON TUESDAY." It was a dim, high-ceilinged, wood-floored chamber, redolent of onions and oranges. A glass case at the back in front of a fortress-like refrigerator room contained a selection of sticks of bologna and salami, a tray of freshly-cut pork chops and a mound of what seemed to be bulk sausage, a crock of cottage cheese, and a hand-written sign promising "Fresh beef cuts and calf's liver available Tuesday." Cardboard cartons with cellophane covers were lined up in a wire rack next to the wooden counter; they contained several kinds of cookies. I noticed molasses cookies with Pepto Bismol-pink icing and ginger-snap windmills particularly; both were favorites of mine. Piles of canned goods brightly labeled for peaches, pears, spinach, peas, and corn stood in consciously architectural array around the centerpiece of a pot-bellied stove. I could imagine the checker games that would replace the canned goods when winter came and the stove was fired up. There was no one about so I finished my inspection and left, vaguely regretting the lost opportunity to buy a bag of windmills. Another time, I told myself.

Going on down the street, I passed Millie's House of Beauty, offering perms and rinses; a barber shop, its pole merrily spinning; a tall 19th century mansion transformed into a funeral home, its gardens converted to a parking lot; two one-story brick buildings side by side, the letters BPOE incised on the concrete lintel over the door of one and the letters IOOF painted on a board over the door of the other. I wondered whether there was a story behind the difference. Beyond the twin brick buildings, the street became strictly residential; modest white frame houses shaded by giant trees stood among carefully tended lawns and flower beds. At the very end of the street, just before cultivated fields took over, there was a ramshackle ice cream stand. It looked barely capable of standing up, much less of serving the public, but a husky young man dressed in overalls was beginning to slap white paint on the front counter. He hailed me.

"You new in town? Staying with Mrs. Pace?"

"Yes and no. Yes, new in town; and no, not with Mrs. Pace. She was full up but found me a room with Madam Anna. Isn't this the wrong time of year to be doing up your stand here?" My reporter's nose smelled another story opportunity.

"I close up for the winter when the Fair opens. Getting a jump on the spring painting. What's your name? Mine's Walt Hawkins."

"Name's Katharine Culhane, going to work for the *Radio Crier.* Speaking of names, do you happen to know how the newspaper got that name?"

"Sure. When my dad, Clint Hawkins, owned it he called it the *Town Crier* but when Sol Baumer bought it, he said it needed a modern twist. So he called it the *Radio Crier.* I think it's kind of a dumb name but considerin' that the news I read in the paper is no worse than what I hear over my radio, I guess it's OK. Say, now that you know about my place here, I hope you'll give it some notice. The *Radio Crier* isn't much of a newspaper but a little free publicity never hurts. I'll be opening first weekend in May."

I said sure and crossed the street to pass by more of the residential areas. I noticed that there was another street of houses one or two short blocks over but I stayed on the main drag to look over more of the downtown commercial places. It was now late enough that almost all were closed for the Fair but I noted them anyway: a jewelry store featuring TIMEX watches in its display window; a dress shop with mannequins sporting rather nice outfits; a shoe store displaying men's and women's shoes and Buster Brown kid's shoes; a restaurant and bakery with a sign, "SEE OUR BOOTH AT THE FAIR." A cross street broke the line of the commercial district, and provided a corner for the location of a two-pump gas station with a repair bay. Half a dozen battered cars were parked on its greasy concrete lot. The *Radio Crier* building came next and then an empty building that showed signs of having been a pool room and exuded odors reminiscent of a beer joint. That was followed by two large barren lots, and then by a store selling hardware, seeds, and John Deere farm implements. This was obviously where I would come for a bicycle. More houses straggled along the roadway, growing more dilapidated the farther the distance from downtown. At the end of the street there was a small office building further dwarfed by three colossal grain elevators towering over it. The complex stood on a railroad spur off the main rail line which crossed the street which was now turning into an asphalted highway. On the opposite side of the street a big, freshly painted sign bearing the legend TYLER COUNTY FAIR and an arrow in red showed the way to the current local attraction. I learned to the sorrow of sore feet that the fairground was four miles farther along the highway. Going to the Fair furthered my education: Prosperity was not the county seat; Columbia, ten miles down the road, was. The county fairgrounds were out in the country due to the pungency of penned-up livestock for a week once a year. I made a mental note that covering country news would be taxing even with a bicycle.

I was lucky enough to hitch a ride back from the fairgrounds to Mrs. Pace's in time for supper. I nevertheless arrived grimy, sweaty, and too full of junk food to do more than pick at Mrs. Pace's cold collation. I hurried through supper and escaped to Madam Anna's and a tepid bath, keeping in mind the shortcomings of the hot water heater. I stretched out briefly on my cot, musing over my day—the exploration of Prosperity, the possibilities of my new job, new people I'd met—mentally selecting and editing what I would record in my journal. But I fell asleep and delayed my write-up until the early hours of Sunday. I had not forgotten a thing but my mental blue pencil had deleted descriptions of the many attractions of the Fair.

❧ 5 ❧

On Sunday morning, I decided to try Wesley Chapel. I wasn't a Methodist but Sol had instructed me to learn the churches and the Chapel was closest, a significant recommendation to my footsore self. I arrived twenty minutes after the service had started and managed to sneak unobtrusively to a seat in the farthest back pew. The congregation was small one, mostly made up of young families. Three or four white-haired couples sat in the front pews, the better to hear what was quite a nice sermon delivered by a portly, red-faced minister. During the closing hymn, *Bringing In The Sheaves* delivered in lusty voices, one of the elderly men rose to take up the collection. I put a 50-cent piece in the plate and was rewarded by the old fellow's singularly sweet smile. After the benediction I rose to leave but was trapped by the nearest parishioner, a young woman lugging a cranky two-year-old, and invited to share cookies and coffee in the fellowship hall. After many introductions and handshakes, many kind words of welcome especially from the pastor, much effort on my part to remember names that matched faces, and two very delicious brownies—I left feeling thoroughly welcomed. I was, however, honest enough to let the folks know I would visit other churches before becoming a regular at any one of them. Armed with carefully-phrased cautions about the shaky positions on faith and finances that I might find elsewhere, I knew writing up church news in Prosperity even if tactfully-worded would be equivalent to traversing a mine field.

I spent the rest of the day tramping the three back streets of the town, getting the street names and house numbers in mind, reading mailboxes and newspaper tubes, and locating another auto repair garage, a small park, and a one-room post office. The newspaper tubes were bright yellow and marked *The Columbian.* I wondered if the *Radio Crier* were distributed to the same boxes. I also wondered who distributed it. (I found out on Saturday as I lugged a canvas bagful of the current issue up and down those streets. And yes, like a cowbird's alien eggs in songbirds' nests, *The Crier* was deposited in *The Columbian*'s yellow tubes.) The back streets were graveled and by the time I had made my exploratory round, I was limping in my thin-soled Sunday shoes. So far my experiences in Prosperity involved a lot of footsoreness. I came back to Madam Anna's house in the early afternoon, wishing Mrs. Pace provided lunch. My walk had generated a big appetite. I made up my mind I would ask Madam Anna if I could keep a supply of cookies in my room in the future. I wondered where she was. I had not seen hide nor hair of her since Friday evening when she had installed me in my room. Today I approached the house from the front. Since the front door was locked, I walked around the side of the house, gawking open-mouthed at an outside wall of tall, wide casement windows standing half-opened. Glimpses of greenery could be seen in the rooms behind them. As I came around the corner to the back yard, I encountered Madam Anna on her knees in a flower bed. She looked up and smiled at my greeting.

"Have you been comfortable in my house?" she said. "I must tell you if you require my attention when you do not see me, please to ring the bell at the kitchen door and I will come. This is my busy season; I'm starting the poinsettias to be ready for the holiday times and potting African violets for my customers in Columbia. I have not intended to neglect you but as I told you, I am unaccustomed to lodgers."

"Oh, do you have a greenhouse?" I wasn't quite sure how to ask my question but she responded immediately.

"No greenhouse, just the rooms on the east side of the house. Would you like to see?"

She rose rather stiffly, dusted off her hands, and led me into a side door that gave on a row of three rooms. The rooms were full of racks and stands of plants. One room was entirely poinsettias in the early stage of their development. Another room displayed those furry-leafed plants that I think are called African violets, some blooming in a riot of colors, others beginning to burgeon into leafy growth. The third room held large pots apparently waiting for plants to be added.

Madam Anna patted the rim of the nearest one fondly and explained, "I will fill these with outdoor plants that I plan to winter over."

I expressed my admiration for her ingenuity in the use of her property to carry on what was clearly a thriving business. She listened graciously and asked if I would enjoy having a particularly gorgeous purple African violet in my room. When I demurred, pleading a black thumb, she told me not to worry, she would care for it so that all I had to do was enjoy the color.

"I bring it up tomorrow after I've watered. Have you enjoyed your exploration of Prosperity so far?"

I thanked her for the violet and assured her of my pleasure in learning my way around the town. I remembered to ask her if I might keep a few cookies in my room for between-meal snacks. Of course, she said. The next day a colorful tin appeared on the bureau in my room; a note stuck to it read "*Für Kuchen.*" Madam Anna's choice of German for her note puzzled me but I shrugged it off. Tuesday, once Hastert's store re-opened, that tin would house cookies. Two days later when I next encountered Madam Anna to thank her I didn't have the nerve to ask about her use of German for the note. Later, after I learned of her extensive language skills, I suspected it was because she wasn't sure of the English spelling of "cookies."

On Sunday afternoon I made the acquaintance of what Madam Anna had so blithely named the "washing apparatus." It consisted of two tubs, one for washing and fitted with a hand-operated agitator and wringer, the other for rinsing. Hoses on hot and cold water taps made filling the tubs easy. Drying was accomplished by hanging the clothes on lines strung at random from the rafters of the basement. I had not had much better facilities in my college dorm so I found these entirely adequate. I made a note to pick up laundry soap at Hastert's when I laid in my store of cookies. The brand I chose was the topic of a popular radio jingle, "DUZ does everything," and indeed it did.

At breakfast the morning of Labor Day, I begged a ride to the fairgrounds. Packing pen and pad in a shoulder bag, I intended to hunt up human interest and color for my next week's stories at the paper. Mrs. Pace took me and Harold to the fairgrounds around 10 A.M. and Curt Dillon made a date to meet me there for the fireworks in the evening and to bring me home. Mrs. Pace's first stop was the craft hall where she found blue ribbons on both her quilt and her tatting. Triumphantly she announced that snooty Miz Prouty had not achieved even an honorable mention on any of her entries. Then Harold and I split, he for the rides and booth games, me for the stock barn. I imagined that 4-H kids would be good story material. In the poultry section I encountered an elderly woman primping a rooster, glowing scarlet and iridescent black. The bird hailed my appearance by crowing so loudly and continuously that I and the old lady could only exchange friendly nods. Farther on I found a teen-ager who was bursting with pride and ill-concealed tears over an enormous pig lolling in the straw of his (her?) pen—pride in the blue ribbon, tears for an imminent parting. His mammoth pet was destined for profitable sale and subsequent conversion to chops and ham in the immediate future. Top dollar per pound was no compensation for his loss but it helped. Another younger kid, leaning on a wire cage in which a sleepy-eyed, flop-eared gray and white rabbit snuggled, described explicit plans for breeding him (her?) to another prize-winner. Next year, an entry to the State Fair competition, at least one offspring would be a sure thing for Top Rabbit. I took notes in detail, I thought, although when I reported to Sol later, he faulted my failure to record genders exactly. I was to remember that sex sells papers. Then I spotted the twinkle in his eye and breathed more easily. I stopped by the farm implement display to marvel at the big tractors and the latest development, a self-propelled combine that cut the wheat, threshed it by means of a mysterious interior process, and spat the grains out into an accompanying truck or wagon bed, all in one operation. The salesman's enthusiasm was infectious. If I had had $15,000, I would have bought one on the spot.

After a dinner of chicken and noodles for fifty cents at the First Baptist Church tent, I went to watch the trotting race, run under the aegis of the First National Bank of Columbia. I noticed surreptitious betting going on under the bleachers and wondered if the bankers knew (or cared) what else their sponsorship supported. Wild enthusiasm prevailed in the stands although the crowd was small. My neighbor on the plank seat accused a new show on the Midway of drawing attendance away. Woman draped in snakes and not much else, he whispered with a leer. After the race, I went to see for myself and decided a flesh-colored body stocking and a strategically arranged boa constrictor provided a limited amount of titillation. I saw Harold, bug-eyed in the crowd, but refrained from admonishing him. In the lofty maturity of my 22 years, I considered gaping at a raree show a rite of passage for an adolescent boy. Supper was spaghetti and meatballs at the Lutheran Church tent (sixty cents) followed by a stroll down the Midway and a rest on the planks set on concrete blocks in the grove next to the glass blower's booth. Dusk brought mounting excitement among the fair-goers and considerable jockeying for best vantage points to watch the fireworks. Curt came along as scheduled and we sat companionably licking our ice cream cones faster than they could melt. The fireworks were glorious—when are fireworks ever not?—and having picked up Harold in the parking lot, Curt drove us home in the gunpowder-scented darkness. It had been a good day and I had a lot to record in my journal. I laid my pad of notes handy for work on Tuesday morning, bathed, and went to bed.

❧ 7 ❦

The following week and months called for a lot of adjustments. First, there were Sol's assignments which ranged from distributing *The Crier* every Saturday afternoon through collecting news from the churches and commercial establishments to attending the sites of the latest barn fires. The fires were generally old news by the time they became grist for *The Crier.* In all the time I worked there we never put out an extra and if breaking news didn't break by Thursday evening, it either didn't make it into the paper or didn't headline in the next issue. That's the way it goes with rural weeklies, I guess. Sally Frye was very helpful when Sol's assignments left me out on a limb. Born and raised in Prosperity, she lived with her widowed mother and had worked for *The Crier* for 25 years. It was she who recommended jeans or Bermuda shorts for bicycle travel. The church ladies won't approve, she said, but they'll get used to it. And it was she who introduced me to the Sears catalog in Laurel Bacon's back room from which we could order the kind of practical clothes that Laurel didn't feature on mannequins in her display window. Sol often sent the two of us out together, she with camera equipment, me with pad and pencil, although she was perfectly capable of both photographing and reporting any occasion. When assignments took us to distant parts of the county, he allowed Sally, but never me, to drive his car. He had a deep distrust of any driver under age 40, but he cheerfully paid the rental for my bicycle.

I collected much of the news on foot, up and down Main Street. I also solicited ads from the stores, but *sub rosa*. It worked this way: I would discover in my news patrol that a shop or business had hot items in the offing, Sally would shoot some useful footage with her camera, then Sol would call up the store or business and offer a nice illustrated ad at a terrific price. Maybe the best name for the procedure would be "super soft-sell advertising." Hastert's supply of packaged mince meat was big the week before Thanksgiving; the shoe store's Back to School Sale of Buster Browns in August; Laurel's latest in ladies' spring hats just before Easter. Of course, there were the "for sale" ads that came over the counter: puppies, cows, ducks, and such; used cars when Hank Costello ran out of space on his lot; special emoluments and enhancements at the beauty parlor right after Millie had returned from a hair fair in Indianapolis. Sally took care of them since she had the most experience in pricing them low enough to woo the business but high enough to at least break even on the paper's production cost. Benjie, the perpetually ink-stained printer's devil, was kept busy working the hand-press on fliers and posters.

Sol wasn't particularly interested in making a profit on *The Crier*. He lived on his retirement from the South Bend Tribune. He ran the *Radio Crier* for fun and an undemanding occupation. His wife was dead, and his son and daughter had scattered to California and Florida, respectively. He was addicted to blistering editorials directed to the shortcomings of the Federal government. If anything in the paper really roused local reaction, it was Sol's take on farm subsidies and the price of gasoline. His viewpoint was never consistent, just insistent. Farm subsidies were saving the agriculture industry one month, corrupting the integrity of the farmer the next month. High-priced gasoline was bankrupting the farmer, but making gas station owners rich. *The Crier* was a cheerful hodgepodge of this and that, hard news downplayed, personalities highlighted, meticulous spelling and grammar enforced. A good bit of its content was cribbed from other newspapers, witness the ragged residues on Sol's desk. Town news was never world-shaking, although the gossip could have been. But, since I was under orders to bring back such pickings back to be vetted by Sol, *The Crier* readership was protected from any embarrassing gaffes I might have committed. "Hmm," Sol would say, "so Walt Hawkins has got the McNabb girl in trouble. Well, we'll just address that with a report that bachelor-about-town Walter Hawkins is spending the winter repairing his ice cream stand, and an item that Sally McNabb, the talented young lady who sings solos at First Baptist services, is taking a year off from college to visit relatives in Kentucky. If we put the two items in adjoining columns of *The Crier*, people will draw their own conclusions with no new damage done to reputations." Then there were the Saturday nights Johnny Card spent in the Columbia poky for being drunk and disorderly in Pete's Bar. One such event was written up as "Johnny Card celebrated his birthday early with friends at a local gathering place." The next time Johnny Card became newsworthy the occasion would be changed to "Fourth of July" or "Lincoln's Birthday" just to let folks know of his frequent binges minus pejorative details. I learned from Sol's euphemisms to get all kinds of news to the population of Prosperity without making enemies. That helped me no end when in years to come I worked as a speech writer for nationally known politicians, men fond of innuendo but leery of libel.

An assignment I especially relished was attendance at the monthly meeting of the village council. It was an experience rich in interesting personalities and topics, and an opportunity to observe democracy in action (actually in slow motion). Mr. Hastert, the grocer, was the current mayor and presided at the table in the IOOF building with a lively gavel and an endless fund of patience. Herman Bergdorf, restauranteur and baker, was immediate past mayor, current vice-mayor, and mayor-elect; he had little to say but stood ready to take the gavel when called on. Debate was usually led by Laurel Bacon's husband, Mac short for Macdougal, who had an opinion of his own or of Laurel's on everything. Bessie Carew, secretary to the council, sat quietly taking voluminous notes, occasionally interrupting to ask someone to repeat himself when in the heat of the moment comment had been rattled off too fast to catch. Voices were often raised and arms waved, many topics were tabled, but Bessie's notes, which as public documents I was allowed to read, were always complete and exact, better than any I could take. The liveliest discussions were, as you may expect, about money—specifically the money allotted by the county for community development. It was, of course, never enough and the county's ideas of community development were consistently at odds with those of the village council. The most frequent source of contention was whether to spend development money on tar or on asphalt to upgrade gravel streets. The thrifty-minded, led by Harry Bender, insisted on tar. The spendthrifts (Harry's epithet) were led by Hank Costello in favor of saving automotive wear and tear. The budget was introduced at the February meeting and was usually passed by May on a unanimous vote, amended by second thoughts in June, again passed to take effect July 1.

Brother John Alder, an elder of the First Baptist Church, sat on the council and acted as its unofficial chaplain, opening and closing each session with a prayer. Issues of separation of church and state didn't bother the good folk of Prosperity, then or ever. Actually the closing prayer was an excellent way to cool tempers and establish a degree of peace before the session broke up. Men in the group often lingered to listen to Will Card, a retired farmer who played an unofficial role as a conduit from the county agent, passing on planting and harvesting ploys and dates, and the latest news of herbicides and fertilizers. Mr. Card was Johnny's long-suffering father, eternally in hopes Johnny would settle down, stay out of Pete's Bar, and apply his talents to scientific farming. I learned a good bit about local agricultural conditions by eavesdropping on these conversations.

During formal deliberations ladies with a bone to pick sat on chairs by the wall, occasionally asking for the floor and venting their concerns. They formed a separate coterie for gossip while Mr. Card was holding forth. I was standing among them when I learned why there was no Mr. Pace at Mrs. Pace's house. Mrs. Pace's rival, that snooty Miz Prouty divulged the story as a cautionary tale, the moral—a woman can only ask so much of her man. Mariah was house-proud, always nagging Frank to pretty up her house and yard—witness the naked lady in the fountain. What could you expect? When the circus came to town and left ten years ago, Frank, who was the local agent for State Farm insurance, ran off with the high wire artist. Mariah was left with that big house and a four-year-old kid, and no means to support either. That was when she started taking lodgers. Miz Prouty expressed some grudging respect that Mariah had made a go of it. I felt almost guilty that I got so much enjoyment out of those council meetings. They were more entertainment than work.

The worst part of working in Prosperity for the next two years was WINTER! Shank's mare was OK for town rounds and the bicycle was OK for fair weather but snow or rain made for heavy going out of town. When I said I had a driver's license, Sol reluctantly looked into renting one of Hank Costello's junkers but that solution was an iffy one at best. Unreliability was the only reliable characteristic of his stock. Heaters that didn't work in winter unstoppably gushed BTUs in the warm summer rains that turned farm roads into bottomless mires. Treadless tires that traveled well enough on dry asphalt highway lost their grip when the pavement was wet or went flat when encountering a stretch of gravel. It was winter that brought me and Madam Anna to a warm and rewarding friendship. She started to watch for my return from a cold, wet day of slogging around on my rounds and to offer me hot milk, fresh-baked bread, and conversation over the scrubbed surface of her kitchen table. Her loneliness surprised me at first, until I learned more of her history. When it came to relationships with family and friends, I found we had a lot in common. Few to none.

❧ 8 ❧

Bit by bit, I pieced together in my own mind a coherent story of Anna's life. Her father was Prince Peter Andreivich Suvorov and she was born on the family estate in Georgia, a province of Imperial Russia. The titles of Prince and Princess didn't mean much in Georgia, she said. Nothing royal in the titles, they were just a custom for an old aristocratic family that had owned land and serfs for several generations. She grew up in the country in the care of governesses and tutors while her beautiful mother and gallant father lived a social whirl in Moscow. Brief winter vacations at an estate in Yalta were the only times she spent with her parents. But when she was 18, her parents brought her to Moscow and put her on the marriage market.

"I was very beautiful then," she said smiling, "and my mother arranged a wardrobe of magnificent gowns for every occasion. Young men struggled with one another to take me driving and to dance with me."

But negotiation after negotiation broke down when the parents of the eligible young men discovered that the Suvorovs, who were up to their ears in debt, could not fund a big dowry for Anna. Approaches by rich old men seeking what we would call in the 21st century a trophy wife collapsed in the face of Anna's adamant refusals to consider them. "I was ready to live

34

unmarried forever rather than marry one of them. They were old, they smelled, and they were probably diseased."

Furious, her parents exiled her to the country estate where she met and fell in love with the scion of a neighboring family, as poor as her own. "He was an officer in the Russian Navy. We saw one another only when he was home on leave. Oh, how much we loved! But not wisely. The baby was passed off as my maid's child. He was beautiful, so big and strong, but he died in his third year."

Speaking of her baby, she wiped tears from her eyes, but she was dry-eyed as she told how her parents had died in the cholera epidemic that swept through Moscow in 1894. Although she was now free to marry her lover, his family balked. The two of them lived in hope and their continuing affair consisted of times he was on leave. When I asked her what she did with her time, she said her education had been very thorough. Her governesses and tutors had taught her to speak, read, and write French, German, and English. The languages opened the world to her since her lover sent her boxes of books from each port where his ship docked. Living in the country gave her a lot of time for gardening and for continuing her education on her own. Their love affair continued until he was killed in the naval action off Tsushima. The next lonely years Anna spent in running the family properties and gardening both out of doors and in the greenhouses she had built on the estate. Then in 1919, the warring armies of the Bolsheviks and Mensheviks swept back and forth across her lands, leaving behind them only fields stripped bare, burned out buildings, and dead people lying on the roadsides.

"I fled from village to village, trying to escape their ravages, using up my money, until I ended up in the Crimea. I was in my 40 years and no longer the beautiful girl. Although I tried to make a living as a translator and interpreter I was often hungry and sometimes homeless."

In Odessa she gained a "protector." From the way she said it, I assumed the protector was a rich and powerful man and she became his mistress. He was very good to her, showered her with fine clothes, jewels, and furs, and finally took her with him to Constantinople, where he was a major figure in the arms trade during the years between the wars. From there, he took her to Paris where she lived until he died in 1930. She arrived in the United States with one steamer trunk, a valise, and a letter from a small college in Ohio offering a position as a foreign language instructor. When she got there the position had been filled. As she sat on her luggage in the bus station, hopelessly contemplating an uncertain future, an elderly man engaged her in conversation. He was kind, interested in her tale, sympathetic to her plight, and ended up inviting her to stay with him in his house in Prosperity until she found work. She accepted and he loaded her trunk and valise into his car. Her American adventure brought her to the house she now owned. The man, widowed and childless, enjoyed her company and when he died just before the war, made her his heir.

"I made a home for him and shared his bed. I am not ashamed for him. It was good for both of us. The people of the town did not approve because we did not marry but after Matthew died, they began to speak friendly, Mariah Pace especially. She has been a good friend."

By the time I had an overall picture of Madam Anna's life, I could understand her reserve. Born to privilege and carefully reared, she had been neglected and betrayed by her parents, then repudiated by them. Her great love having been thwarted of consummation, she finally had to depend, simply to survive, on old men the likes of which she once spurned. I had to admire the serenity with which she related the ugly side of her life, and the courage with which she had faced its challenges. I could see why she loved plants. They never played her false, never demanded pay for the color they added to her life.

I discovered the secret of her erect posture by chance. In the third year after I arrived in Prosperity, I came home late one winter afternoon, soaked to the skin by an ugly, sleety rain. I intended to take a bath to warm up before going to supper at Mariah Pace's bountiful table. I was in my robe and slippers when I opened the bathroom door and found Madam Anna in her underclothes sprawled on the floor in a kind of cocoon of bath towels. She was lying very still, breathing heavily, and I feared she had had a stroke. But when I called her name, she replied at once to tell me that she was all right; she had fallen and been unable to get up. As I bent over her, intending to take her arms and assist her to her feet, I saw a contraption of leather and metal lying on a chair.

"My brace," she said. "I came to bathe so I took it off. Then I fell and couldn't get up again."

"When did this happen? Should I call a doctor for you? Do you think you broke anything?"

"No, I came to bathe about two o'clock. I've been on the floor since then but towels I pulled out of the cabinet kept me from cold. No doctor. Nothing broke. If you help me, I can get the brace on and then I'll be able to get up."

"How can we do that? I really think I need to call Mariah and get her to help."

"No, don't bother anyone. Just lay the brace out on the floor in a way I will tell you and I will roll over into it."

I followed her instructions to position the straps and metal bands, then assisted her to roll on to them. Then she and I pulled on the straps and adjusted the bands until she was encased in the brace from hips to chest. Once everything was in proper place and properly secured, she had me pull the chair to her and to steady it while she worked herself upright across the seat. When she was on her feet again, she sat down and drew long breaths of exhaustion.

"Are you sure no doctor? Nothing broken? You haven't had your bath. Can I help you...."

"No doctor." She was firm. "Nothing broken. I take a bath tomorrow after I have rested. Thank you very much. I was foolish to have the chair too far from the tub when I took off the brace. I usually manage very well. It is good that you stay here; I might have been on the floor for a very long time before I could crawl down the stairs to phone Mariah. I thank you very much. Please not to worry about me."

I helped her put on her slippers and shrug into her robe. She apologized for taking so long to get ready to go downstairs. Then she told me the reason for the brace, a spinal injury occurring a year or so after Matthew's death. The doctors wanted to operate but she couldn't afford it and the doctors couldn't guarantee good results. Therefore the brace. Ordinarily she took it off and on while lying in bed or sitting on the chair in the bathroom.

"But I am foolish and careless today. I must be more careful from now on. I am so sorry to impose on you."

I reassured her and proceeded to escort her downstairs to her bedroom, a chamber even more austere than mine had been when I took up lodgings in it. As I left her, she called after me,

"A mail came for you. I mean, a letter came. I put it on the hall table."

The letter was in response to an application I had made for a position on Bennett Carver's staff. Carver was the local incumbent of a seat in the House of Representatives and going all out in a push for re-election. He felt his campaign needed a boost from some lively speeches. The chairman of his campaign had approached me, saying the campaign committee liked what they read in *The Crier* under my by-line, and urging me to submit an application. If Carver's run for the House was successful, he would be taking his staff with him to Washington, D.C. The salary would be three times what Sol Baumer could pay and the experience would be a golden addition to my résumé. Of course, there was the possibility that Carver's run might be unsuccessful and I would have lost my now comfortable niche on *The Crier* and be without a job. Accepting the job offer came with a risk. And leaving the people I had come to know and like better than my own blood kin would not be easy. I had to do some heavy thinking about it.

INTERLUDE
1955-2000

1955

Bennett Carver was re-elected to the House of Representatives and leaving Prosperity behind me, I went with his staff to Washington, D.C. It was the beginning of a career that I, as a callow 22-year old, could never have imagined. I grew older and more cynical and more affluent and less trusting and less pretty and less a lot of things. Not long after my advent in Washington, I gave up writing my journal. I would not take it up again for some years. Madam Anna and I exchanged postcards from time to time, the kind that read "How are you? I'm fine," and not much else. I occasionally felt a pang of regret that I hadn't made a visit back to Prosperity to see how my friends were doing but the press of my busy life quickly stifled any guilt. Out of sight, out of mind—that became my mantra. Living in Washington began and completed the loss of my innocence. The picture in my college yearbook had shown me blonde, with sparkling blue eyes and a peach-blow complexion. The caption listed all my collegiate triumphs: honoraries, merit scholarships, class rank. The comment read "will make some lucky guy happy," the inference being "in marriage." Well, I had let a couple of guys get lucky but not in marriage. High school and college yearbooks in that era never considered that possibility. Furthermore, there was never a word about how a woman made a go of it in a man's world. But I was out to try.

From being Carver's speech writer, I moved to the staff of

Senator Brant Hale and got involved in an amorous fling with another senator; I wrote speeches for Hale for a few years and escaped from my involvement with his colleague without major damage to my self-esteem. By the time I had forged a lot of contacts on the Hill, my talents had become a prized commodity at *The Washington News* and I was teamed up with Gordon Clavering on an investigative reporting beat. We pulled off three reportorial coups, one of which brought down a racist Cabinet nominee from a deep South state. I had achieved considerable stature in my profession and a certain smug satisfaction with the degree of my success.

1961

Then I fell head over heels in love with Pierre DeNeuve, star correspondent for *Agence Presse*. I broke the lease on my apartment, put the contents into storage, and followed Pierre to Paris without benefit (or curse) of marriage. Nevertheless, our life was fantastic. We lived on the fifth floor of an 18th century building with 15th century plumbing, employed the inept services of a dim-witted maid, and ate our meals in the neighborhood bistros. Our congerie of friends included writers, actors, painters, poets, playwrights, a medical student or two, at least one con man—most of them poor but all rich in wit, imagination, and intellectual energy. We often sat into the wee hours talking, laughing, singing, drinking, and dreaming out loud. I added to our income by doing features for the international editions of major American papers. Four deliriously happy years with Pierre passed before he informed me he had fallen out of love with me and into love with a famous fashion model. It came as a shock, I had been sure my life was bullet proof.

I met Elizabeth Fritz at the American Embassy not long after Pierre moved out. I was covering an occasion to which a number of Americans temporarily in France had been invited. She and I fell into one of those cocktail conversations about everything and nothing. She was looking for a place to live while she spent a sabbatical at the Sorbonne. I was lonely and depressed living in a place where both Pierre and happiness had deserted me. I invited her to share the apartment and we hit it off immediately. Our friendship lasted for many years despite long gaps between actual contacts. We built it on the considerable free time each of us had at the time in Paris. I enjoyed introducing her to my friends and favorite haunts. She in turn introduced me to her project: a book on the development of modern concepts of biochemistry from Pasteur and Ehrlich to the molecular level of Watson and Crick. Biochemistry was a mystery for me but Elizabeth's explanations made it vital, interesting, and intriguing. As I describe it, I almost feel I should capitalize the adjectives. What I learned led to several publishable and profitable articles for the popular scientific press. I owe Elizabeth the ability I have to appreciate biology and I am not ashamed to say she owes me a working knowledge of French, although she never did get the hang of pronunciation.

Bess, as she invited me to call her, and I trudged together from one dingy 19th century laboratory to another, as well as up and down the stairs of elderly and modern scientific establishments. We also absorbed vast amounts of French culture. Bess had an insatiable interest in the new architecture and constructions that had covered up ancient cityscapes and modified those that survived, and in the social adjustments that the population had made and *not* made to the influence that modernization had had on art and literature. She was the first and only intimate friend I had ever had. We had great fun together. She educated me far more than any college course I had ever taken and I will be forever grateful to her for it. We kept up a desultory correspondence for years after her sabbatical ended. Long may she live and thrive!

1965

After a year in France Bess returned to America and I was living alone again. The circle of friends in which Pierre and I had moved now seemed boring and trivial and I drifted away from them. Lonesome and solitary I began to spend my free time brooding. The pain of Pierre's rejection resurfaced and occupied my thoughts. I fell into a deep depression not relieved by alcohol or a succession of powerful anti-depressants. Although the international papers occasionally took some of my pieces, I found it difficult to work. I continued free-lancing, but found no great call for my stories. I used up most of my savings and a lot of my credit with my colleagues in the press. I'm not proud of my life in those years. It was loveless, sterile, dull, and lasted too long.

One day I packed up two suitcases and my typewriter in my tiny little Peugeot and headed away from Paris going nowhere special, just somewhere else. The car broke down in a dusty little backwater in Provence. The local mechanic looked under the hood, shook his head, and sucked his teeth in despair. I finally got him to say he would try to get it running again and

I took a room over a café that stood on the Place Garibaldi. There was absolutely nothing to do in Donzieres—it was that kind of a village, no movie house, no library—so I walked in the cool of the morning in the hills and paced the streets in the warm twilight, and sat looking out over the hot, sun-struck plaza in the afternoon when most of the populace napped in the cool dark of their houses. By the end of a week the mechanic had given up, I had traded the car for his repair bill, and the heat and peace of Donzieres's stone and stucco had penetrated deep into my heart and mind. It healed me of Pierre, of unrequited love, of failure, and of depression. I still had some money, so I put a baguette, a jar of paté, and a bottle of wine in my back pack, entrusted my suitcases and typewriter temporarily to my landlord and set out to roam the hills. I wasn't sure what I was looking for but I figured I'd know it when I stumbled over it.

What I found was Madame Marie Delon's goat farm. It sat on the brow of a sun-seared hill overlooking a valley through which a perpetual brook flowed from a spring in a crevice in the hill. The valley was green and fresh even in the worst heat of the summer, a rarity in the Midi, and Madame Marie's goats thrived on it. She herded them out to green pastures every morning and herded them home every evening. We negotiated lodging and I trudged back to the village for my suitcases and typewriter. She charged me 25 francs a week for board (mostly goat milk, cheese, and vegetables) and room (a rickety lean-to on her 300-year-old, two-room stone cottage). I could walk to Donzieres in an hour or so for whatever else I needed and might be found there. For an extra five francs Madame Marie did my laundry, scrubbing it vigorously with her gnarled brown hands on a washboard propped in a tub, spreading it to dry on the bushes in the sun or draping it around the kitchen when the mistral blew. She was a garrulous old lady, white-haired, with beady black eyes, clad in rusty black, as quick on her feet as one of her goats. The first World War had made her a widow, the second had killed her two sons. Although she spoke perfectly good French when she meant me to understand her, she seemed to prefer mystifying me with patois most of the time. She was a woman who wanted to maintain the upper hand all the time, whether over goats or a lodger.

I spent three months on Madame Marie's hilltop, but moved on when winter and the mistral made life in her lean-to miserable. I hiked down to Donzieres, loaded myself and my stuff on the bus, and headed for Italy. I was carrying in one of my suitcases the draft of a novel loosely based on events that had touched Madame Marie's life. I got to Italy by fits and starts, financing my journey with travel pieces for an American magazine the editor of which was an old acquaintance. I ran a gamut from Avignon (Palace of the Popes) to Monaco (the Casino) to Genoa (the Columbus memorial) to Sicily (the cathedrals of Palermo) and finally to Rome (for any monument that would stand still long enough for a word portrait). Dreaming one day on the Spanish Steps, I looked up to see one of the old crowd from the Paris days. She had become the Principessa di Gordiani, known to me more familiarly as Kitty. She invited me home to her palazzo and I accepted, hoping for modern plumbing. In fact, her palazzo had been converted into apartments and thoroughly modernized. She was off to spend her winter in Florida, Fort Lauderdale to be specific, and asked me to house sit. I accepted with alacrity and got to work getting my novel into a publishable state. I had titled it "*Where Are My Sons?*" and had explored the theme of the two generations of young men decimated by war, not just Madame Marie's husband and sons but the husbands and sons of all the women of Europe. I ended up house sitting for Kitty for three years—just enough time for her to meet and marry an American, *nouveau riche* from computer software, bear him a child, and then divorce him, the richer by a munificent settlement on her and her son. I had had time to finish my "Sons" and submit it to two successive publishers and to start a second novel (not yet titled), a romance set in Rome. Kitty, her son, and his nurse returned in July, spent two days in hot and humid Rome, then headed for Gstaad.

1969

I was still in residence in the palazzo but realized my days there were numbered. I took a cheap apartment in a jerry-built government-sponsored housing development and submitted the "Sons" to the third publisher, an American house. He bought it, provided an advance of a hundred thousand dollars, and suggested I return to the U.S. to do the promotion. I acquired an agent and before long the book was in paperback and the movie rights were acquired by MGM. I went to California to participate in writing the screenplay. Participate is a euphemism for standing by while a studio hack cut the heart out of my book as a means to put it on the silver screen. But even disenchantment pays well in Hollywood.

1970

To tide over my finances while I was in Rome I had tossed off a romance novel or two, lots of steamy sex in exotic milieus, the kind of novel that generated lurid dust jackets on hard cover books and even more lurid covers on paperbacks. My trashy novels had proved very popular with a publisher more interested in quantity of sales than in quality of content, and he promoted them to a public that ate 'em up. I recalled Sol Baumer's maxim that sex sells newspapers; I'm here to tell you sex sells books even faster. I was sufficiently ashamed of them—they were tawdry, trivial, and trite—that I employed a *nom de plume* that I protected fiercely from disclosure. But they were easy to write, they made a lot of money, and I turned them out like pancakes in the church tent at the Tyler County Fair. Occasionally, I placed my plot in a historical frame; the research in these instances motivated me to write some serious historical non-fiction. I did a book on Father Junipero Serra and the string of missions he built along the spine of California. It was titled "*Serra, Servant of God*" and ended up on the *New York Times* Top Ten non-fiction list four weeks in a row. Its success inspired me to work on another, a political history of Hong Kong. I was doing so well financially that I invested in a property in Malibu and engaged a Filipino couple, Luz and Ramon Morenas, to keep it.

1975

The house in Malibu was large, airy, and almost too modern. Once the interior decorator had finished with it, it seemed bare and cold. I remembered then that I had been paying storage bills for years on stuff I had stored in Washington. The annual bills had followed me around my peripatetic life and I had always managed to pay them. Somewhere in my subconscious I think I imagined the stored items as anchors tying my disorganized and rootless present to a stable past. The apartment I closed in Washington in order to go to Paris and live with Pierre had a wire cage in the basement into which I had put the accumulation of my youth. When my grandparents were killed, my mother, being the sole heir, had come to Kansas to settle the estate. The farm was heavily mortgaged and didn't bring much but what there was my mother dedicated to my college education. She sold up most of the household goods but selected what she called "worthwhile family pieces" and arranged with a neighbor to store them in his attic until she or I would want them. Among the items was a pair of matching Windsor chairs that Mom said had belonged to her grandparents and a chest-on-chest-on-chest that my grandfather had bought at a sale. Mom grew enthusiastic about it—said it was Shaker work, and being three-tiered, very rare and worth a lot of money. She wished she had a place for it in her and the Colonel's quarters on base in the Canal Zone. There was also a nice little gate-legged table and a marble-topped sideboard. As a child, I had looked on that sideboard as the source of all good things; Grandma kept the hard candy locked in one of the drawers, the key in her apron pocket. Another drawer held a treasure trove of simple toys that I was allowed to play with on special occasions—a top, a mechanical bank, a whirligig. Mom said they were Grandpa's toys when he was a little boy. Mom bundled the nice china and crystal pieces that had been Grandma's pride and joy in shredded newspaper and boxed it up. Other boxes were filled with family papers and photographs. In 1960, the last year I spent in Washington, the old neighbor informed my mother he was selling up the farm and moving to town. What did she want to do with the stuff in his attic?

Mom paid to have the stuff sent to me; she had no room for it now that she and the General were living in Brussels. Neither did I in my apartment, but the cage in the basement of the apartment building was big enough to hold it. I never opened the boxes. When I left Washington, I had the movers put them into storage along with the current contents of the apartment. That was in 1961 and now in 1978, discontented with the barren look of my super-modern house, I remembered those things and saw no reason to keep on paying to store them. I sent for them and had them placed in the big basement of the Malibu house. I unpacked the furniture and found places for it in the living areas upstairs. But there was a lot more stuff to go through and I told myself I'd get to it one of these days.

One item came as a surprise to me. It was an old-fashioned steamer trunk, labeled with my Washington address and marked from "Suvorov, 102 Elm Street, Prosperity, Indiana." I was at a loss to explain how or when I had come by it but a shipping tag still affixed to the trunk bore a date about a week before I took off for Paris. I remembered that morning, the movers were still in the house and I was late, about to miss my plane, so I left everything in their hands. After I had gone and before they had finished, the trunk must have been delivered and they just put it with the other stuff they were storing. When I tried the latches, I found the trunk locked and without a key, I would have to engage a locksmith to open it. Then my publisher called to badger me to finish the Hong Kong book and I had to go to Hong Kong to complete the research. I put opening the trunk on the back burner and forgot it.

1980

My mother died of a heart attack in while I was in Hong Kong. She was 76 and I had not seen her since we cleared out my grandparents' things years ago. The General sent me a note with a few details of Mom's death and a package containing the leather box in which she kept her jewelry. The General said he was keeping those pieces of jewelry he had given her. The odds and ends in the box included an antique brooch Grandma used to wear, some simple gold chains, a coral and crystal necklace, a gold bracelet, and Mom's wedding and engagement rings from her first marriage. Turning the engagement ring in my hand I recalled a cruel joke she had made as she showed it to me when we were going over my grandparents' things. "This is the Culhane Cullinan, a memento of your father," she said with a bitter smile. I didn't know it was a joke at the time, not until I read a National Geographic article about historic gemstones. My parents' marriage must have been very unhappy and the parting far from amicable. But the way they chose to live their lives made their existence tangential to mine and their unhappiness did not sadden me. Over the years, when I thought of my childhood and my parents and grandparents, I made few judgments—my parents were irrelevant, my grandparents were relevant. My parents weren't there, my grandparents were. Even now, fingering mementoes of my mother's life, I felt no sentimental attachment to her.

1985

The Hong Kong book had come out in a flurry requiring travel for book signings, TV and newspaper interviews, and full page ads in trade magazines. But after a year on the road, I called the hoopla quits. Spectacular sales and fat royalties were no compensation for my exhaustion. I retreated to Malibu for R and R, lazy days poolside basking in the sun, potting about barefoot in the flower beds the gardener allowed me to desecrate. But even R and R can pall and I rather welcomed the invitation to the wine-and-cheese opening of a photography retrospective, life work of a single-syllable virtuoso of the Hasselblad. The banner over the gallery door read "Photos By Blink." I groaned, cutesy wasn't up my alley but I had put on heels and my best underwear and it was too late to turn around and go home. Once inside, I was blown away by the photos; they were wonderful. Those in black and white were particularly powerful, and one, the image of a Serbian child squatting at the side of his dead mother, seemed to imprint on the inside of my eyelids.

"Come meet the artist," the host said, taking me by the elbow and towing me over to a tall, white-haired, white-bearded man leaning on a cane. There was something faintly familiar in the dark eyes that locked on mine.

"This is the famous author, Katharine Culhane. You were just saying the other day how perceptive you found her latest book, *A Hong Kong For the Ages*." The host dropped me off and walked away, leaving me with nothing to say to this perfect stranger. So I said,

"I'm awed by your work. So powerful, so true. Tell me. How did you come to be called 'Blink'?"

"I didn't come to be at all," was the tart response. "Not my idea. An overenthusiastic publicist decided a single-syllable appellation would be more memorable than my own pedestrian name. I went along, path of least resistance, you know. The publicist had picked up on something I had said in an interview. 'Blink and what you see is gone, capture it on film and you've got something to carry away'. Say, Ms. Culhane, could we be related? My name is really Brian Culhane although I've always signed the work offered for sale as B. C."

I felt my face go white and my knees grow wobbly. My dad? I couldn't remember when I had seen him last, maybe when I was 12 or 13? This old man white-headed, leaning on a cane? I sank onto a convenient bench to catch my breath.

"Are you OK? I didn't mean to shock you. I hope you aren't insulted. But are you by any chance my daughter Katharine? Lived in Kansas with the Webers, your grandparents? Your mother's name was Lola maybe?"

He was so casual, so offhand, that I opted to react in kind.

"All that is hardly coincidence. The last time I remember seeing you was 1942 or 1943. You came by my grandparents' house to pick up some of your stuff. My grandma said she was glad my mom wasn't there."

"Yes, Lola and I … well, in spite of the divorce, we still had unresolved issues. Lots of hurt all the way around. But that's all in the past. Would you be interested in getting to know one another?" His voice and manner were hesitant. "I don't want to impose. Your mother probably gave me a bad rep and I confess to neglecting you but it was wartime and a lot of things fell through the cracks. I regret that now. I know I can't make up for old hurts but I'd…."

I interrupted to say, "Sure, sure. OK. Give me a call." And I scribbled my number on the back of one of the cards lying on a side table. Just then, the host shepherded an obviously affluent couple up to meet him, and with a sidelong glance at me, he tucked the card in his vest pocket and turned to talk with them. I hastened to escape. It would take me some time and distance to absorb this latest twist in my life.

Several weeks later, he called and I invited him to dinner. Luz and Ramon pulled out all the stops when they learned he was my long-lost father. They were firm believers in family ties, making them, maintaining them, and restoring those that had dropped by the wayside. The atmosphere was rather strained during our pre-dinner drinks, but developed into civilized conversation with wine at dinner. When we repaired to the living room after dinner, it was brandy and coffee that dispelled the strain at last. I shifted the onus of further conversation to him,

"Why don't you begin at the beginning and tell me about your life? I felt that I was reading an autobiography in your photography but I'm interested in the man who was behind the lens." A clumsy opening but it worked. Long experience had taught me every man, especially a successful man, loves to talk about himself.

He began with his experience as a combat photographer in WW II, in the Italian campaign with the American forces and then in the Greek Civil War with the British advisors. After the war, he worked for CARE around the world, focusing on the children orphaned and displaced by the social disruption of war. Many of his shots were used in the organization's fund-raising efforts. Korea and Viet Nam were other stops on his world wide travels. In the five years he spent in Viet Nam, he met and married a Viet Namese girl who died in childbirth along with their child. He spoke of her with genuine sadness. He never lacked for takers when he offered his photos for sale and that led to a modest degree of financial security. Consequently, he had been able to concentrate in recent years on photographic artistry. He was especially pleased that the pieces in the room devoted to his latest work at the retrospective had had such a favorable reception. Looking up at a broad expanse of bare wall in my living room, he interrupted his story to say, "As soon as I dismantle this show, I hope you will look through the black and white landscapes and select one you like for a place on that wall. Having seen your house, I won't volunteer either documentary or color photos. They simply wouldn't go here. What do you say?"

"I'd be honored to have your work on my wall. I was awed at the breadth and depth of feeling your pictures displayed."

Maybe it was the brandy, or maybe it was the humanity I had glimpsed as he talked, but I was beginning to feel a bond with him. Not a father-daughter bond, but a friend-to-friend connection. When he turned from his biographical narration to elicit mine, I was comfortable relating my experiences, successes, and a few of the failures. Neither of us had dwelt on the feelings or emotions, or perhaps the recriminations, that hid behind forty some years of estrangement. But after I had bid him good-bye and gone off to bed, I did some hard thinking. I concluded that seeing more of him would be no bad thing.

Over the next few months we saw each other frequently and shared a lot about our lives. Only once did he refer to his differences with my mom.

"I was a clerk in a camera shop when we married. Lola was bright, ambitious, and energetic; she wanted me to succeed at something. In the end, she was eating me alive. I escaped into the service and she into government work. Our mismatch produced you and of course, I was out of the picture. That was the way Lola wanted it. But after she met her military man, an officer on the way up, maybe she or he was just as happy to leave you with the Webers. Now that I know you, I think they did a good job of raising you."

I had selected the photograph I wanted from his show. It was an oblong about two feet tall and three feet wide, a snow scene of leafless trees on a slope, all black or white except for a fox, his body russet, his pose alert but half buried in the snow, waiting and watching. I found in it a paradigm of my life. Brian approved of my choice.

"You've got a good eye," he said. "I had to have that printed by a special process to get it that large. It turned out well, I thought."

1988

Brendan came into my life as Brian was leaving it. The last months of Brian's life he spent in my guest house with a full-time male nurse. A stroke had left him helpless, unable to care for himself. Luz and Ramon cheerfully carried his and the nurse's meals from the house and equally cheerfully added the cleaning and laundry chores of the guest house to their routine tasks. They approved whole-heartedly of my care for Brian; in their minds, family took care of family, whatever the circumstances. Brian had lost his ability to talk but when we sat together, his hand in mine, his eyes communicated love. It came late but it came and that was all I needed. He died just before Christmas. Before his stroke, he had written a long testament and left it with his lawyer. It provided for the disposal of his remains, whether physical, professional, or artistic. Cameras, lenses, and accessory equipment were to be donated to a university photojournalism program. His photo collection and negatives were to go to the Smithsonian, except for any prints that I might choose to keep. His savings were to go to the *Save the Children Fund*; they made a respectable contribution. I saw his ashes into the columbarium at Forest Park and went occasionally to visit, not to mourn, just to be there for a few quiet minutes.

I met Brendan as I was packing up Brian's household goods prior to moving him to my guest house. Brendan lived in the apartment next to Brian's and the two of them had made a habit of attending concerts, plays, and exhibitions together. I gave Brian's big old leather Laz-Z-Boy to Brendan as a memento of his companionable visits to Brian's apartment. Brendan then came to visit Brian in the guest house from time to time and would often stop by the main house for coffee and a chat. We discovered that we had moved in the same circle years ago in Paris. Although neither of us remembered the other very well, we both remembered mutual acquaintances. Our casual re-acquaintance blossomed into relaxed companionship. I spent an occasional weekend at his place, or he came to mine, or we went together to Big Sur or Palm Springs. He was an accomplished lover and after long years of celibacy, I relished his attentions. He asked me several times to marry him but I refused. I was too satisfied with my totally independent way of living. When my refusals failed to drive him away, I ended up with the best of two worlds—my independence and an undemanding bed partner. Our relationship trudged along for nine or ten years and ended amicably when Brendan went to live with his married daughter in Ireland. We joked that he was reversing his namesake's westward journey, in an airplane rather than a leather curragh.

I was still writing sleazy romance novels between serious

historical works. The romance novels were so easy, they just sort of flowed out effortlessly, and equally effortlessly found a friendly reception with my publisher. He called me the "doyenne of his romantic list," a title I found of dubious value. My true identity had leaked out but I still published the romance stuff under the name of M.J. Cuthbert. Thankfully, disclosure of my *nom de plume*'s true name had not injured the esteem of publishers for my serious books. These days I worked on biography a good bit. Research for bios of Zebulon Pike and John Wesley Powell made separate books and developed a nice continuum of the history of Western exploration in the 19th century. Both books were well-received.

2000

I arrived at the millennium in my 72nd year, reasonably healthy, happy enough, comfortably well off, but vaguely discontented. I felt I was leaving some important things undone. I decided that one project still undone was unpacking and sorting the memorabilia (or junk?) recovered from the storage company and still sitting in my basement. I started on it one Saturday morning.

The first box I opened was a storehouse of Weber papers and photographs. The papers were interesting: the farm records; birth, baptismal, and confirmation certificates for both grandparents, my mother, and me; carefully clipped newspaper articles that recorded what were world-shaking events for Kansas farm folk. The headlines chronicled Armistice, 1914; FDR's declaration of the bank holiday; the Japanese attack on Pearl Harbor; and the end of WW II. Other clippings included my parents' wedding picture, stories of their departures for war duties, and announcements of my small triumphs in grade and high school. The newspapers and clippings Grandma had saved were yellowed and so brittle that they shattered in my hands. The photos in albums had been carefully labeled with the names of people I had never heard of. Packages of loose photos that had melted into each other were irrecoverable. However, I rescued and repacked whatever had survived.

The next two boxes contained crystal side dishes and bowls, or more likely cut glass, since crystal was uncommon in a bare subsistence Kansas farmhouse. Some of the china in the boxes was quite pretty, but most of it was mismatched survivors of long-gone sets. I selected some of the most attractive dishes for display upstairs in the living and dining rooms. Opening a flannel bundle of horribly tarnished silverware, I found a complete set of eight place settings. Hallmarks and the initial C seemed to indicate my mother's wedding silver; I packaged it up to take to a restorer. More boxes contained clothing, shoes, books, and knickknacks from my Washington apartment. The clothing would go to a little theatre group that was always hard up for period costumes, the books would go upstairs to my library, and the knickknacks—most of them pointless trash that once meant something—well, I boxed them up with the intention to visit them later. In the box of books, I found the journals I had written in Prosperity and I set them aside to read later. That left the steamer trunk that Madam Anna had sent me. I went upstairs to call a locksmith. When he couldn't come for two more days, I left everything and went for a swim.

A week later, the locksmith had been and gone. I got around to tackling the crumbling leather straps and tarnished buckles of the trunk, and opened it, releasing a strong odor of camphor.

The trunk was the kind that stood on one end and opened into two sections, one fitted with drawers, the other with hangers. The clothing in the hanger side was shrouded in linen covers. Removing them I found gowns in the high style of the 20s and 30s: fabrics of heavy satin, silk, and faille, richly decorated with glass or jet beads, or seed pearls, or gold (somewhat tarnished) braid or fringe. They were so beautiful they took my breath away. Who would have thought that Madam Anna possessed such magnificent attire? I recalled her wearing washed-off denim shirts and bulky dark skirts, a far cry from what must have been the clothing of her Paris days. I turned to the drawers and opened the top one first, to disclose hats, again high style, flowers, fruit, feathers, gossamer veils; and elegant, hand-made shoes carefully bundled in linen bags. The second drawer was stuffed with a fur I didn't recognize, sable perhaps. The garment came out with some difficulty; surprisingly it was stiff as well as bulky. It turned out to be a jacket or stole wrapped around something flat and solid. The flat, solid thing was an icon of the Virgin, painted on a fine-grained, light-colored wood, framed in heavy gold, about 12 by 15 inches in size. The frame was studded with red, green, and blue stones which I assumed were gems. All I knew of icons was what I had read in a cover story of the National Geographic magazine a few years back. This one looked authentic and valuable. It had such astounding beauty that I sat turning it my hands for minutes before laying it aside to try the next drawer. More fur, a coat or cape this time. When I took it out, a small object fell out of it. The object was an oval piece about two inches across, ivory with a painting of a very beautiful young woman in a low-cut gown. I thought I detected a resemblance to Madam Anna's face as I remembered it. A relic of her youth, perhaps? Another treasure to lay aside. The bottom drawer held more fur and another icon, this one as ornate as the first but seemingly much older and rather smaller. The wood backing was stained dark with age, the frame was as richly ornamented but more extensive; it covered the whole icon leaving only a window for the face of the saint (I assumed it was a saint, the Virgin would hardly wear a beard). Again the item was astounding in its rich, dark beauty. There were certainly Customs regulations in force when Madam Anna arrived in the U.S.; she must have smuggled the icons into the country, gambling on a Customs officer too lazy to haul out all of her furs. Having emptied all of the drawers, I noticed that the lining of the fourth drawer was somewhat rumpled; when I picked at it with a fingernail, it peeled away to disclose a folded sheet of paper. In Madam Ann's careful handwriting, I read:

Caterina

These things are for you. You were good in my life. Maybe something bad will happen to me and you will save these things from my life.

Anna Petrovna Suvorov

Tears came quickly. To be called "good in my life" was a great tribute. Madam Anna had been good in my life too, but I had never told her so. Now, many of my tears arose from guilt. Why had I not kept in better touch with her? Youth is selfish but mine was more selfish than most, I had to admit. I hadn't even noticed that there were no more postcards to answer after I had gone haring off to Paris with Pierre. Then another bit of her note struck me. Had something bad happened to her? Is that why there were no more postcards? Knowing that she was already old when I first knew her, I also knew that this was a communication from the grave. I would make a visit to Prosperity, sit for a little while by her grave, and leave flowers on it.

RETURN TO PROSPERITY

CHAPTER NINE

I wound up outstanding engagements, had the Mercedes serviced, and started out for Indiana. Luz and Ramon were all bent out of shape that I would be driving alone all that distance. What if something happened? Who would look after me? I finally convinced them nothing would happen and I would call them at every overnight stop on the way. The two of them stood on the front steps wringing their hands as I started out on a Monday morning in April. The trip was entirely uneventful; I actually enjoyed it. Lots of Public Radio stations to tune into, good driving weather, comfortable Marriott Inns for overnight stays, pretty good food in their dining rooms. My calls to Luz and Ramon were genuinely upbeat.

I arrived in Prosperity on a Thursday evening, wondering if the paper was still put to bed at 11 P.M. I had reserved accommodations at a highly recommended bed-and-breakfast called The Nook. It was located on the road to Columbia, just past the fairgrounds, an old farmhouse tricked out in fresh paint, restored gingerbread, and creative landscaping. My room was furnished in Victorian clutter and lots of floral chintz. I smiled remembering the stark bedchamber into which Madam Anna had ushered me fifty years ago. The bed was wonderfully more comfortable than that long ago cot, the hot water in the bathroom was absolutely inexhaustible, and the wall-to-wall carpet was definitely cozier than the bare wood floor I remembered.

I unpacked my laptop computer and set it up on an ornately carved table that served as a desk. Then I sat down and wrote up my journal before bed. Yes, I had picked up the habit again in the years I was traveling around on book tours. The entries lacked the naiveté and freshness of those I had penned in my spiral notebook so long ago. But then, so did I. Having written up today's arrival, I sat leaning my head on my hand, remembering, until I brought myself up with a jerk. Opening the window wide, I drew in great draughts of spring-scented air and reminded myself I had to get down to business, live in the here and now. I would start in the morning to explore Prosperity 2000.

CHAPTER TEN

I rose early, commanded by a screeching blue jay teetering on a tree branch just outside my window. Fortunately my hostess was also an early riser, but regrettably a mediocre cook. After a breakfast which in no way equaled the Mariah Pace products I remembered, I started out in the car. My first encounter with major changes was the Wal-Mart that now sprawled in a vast parking lot next to the fairgrounds which had turned into a grassy field, all the buildings gone, not even ruins left to mark the former use. Continuing to Prosperity, I found both sides of the road lined with housing developments: neat little brick-and-shingle houses on winding streets, accessed by carefully landscaped entrances marked with names like WillowWood (no sign of a willow) and Covington Cove (no sign of water), signs of the times. The grain silos still stood on the other side of the railroad, the little office boarded up, the towers needing paint but apparently still in use. Main Street was still wide, marked for diagonal parking in front of most of the buildings I remembered. At this hour the street was as deserted as it had been on Fair Day 50 years ago, but it did show evidence of use, grease and oil splotches marking most of the parking slots. Mariah Pace's house stood foursquare on its fine lawn, its wide front porch still populated with white rocking chairs. The fountain with the naked lady was somewhat the worse for wear. The lady had lost an arm although the one holding the urn was still poised coquettishly over her head.

The *Radio Crier* building was gone, Hastert's grocery had been transformed into an artsy-tartsy Hallmark store, the beauty shop was now Celine's, the barber pole didn't spin any more, the funeral home had been renamed but everything else about it had stayed the same. The BPOE building still stood, a sign out front touting a Jonah Fish Fry, Fryday at Five. Its twin had lost the IOOF sign but had gained a big window in its brick façade where gold leaf proclaimed it the Prosperity City Hall and Visitor Center. Walt Hawkins's ice cream stand was gone and the fields next to it were planted with more houses, these larger and pricier (I guessed) than those on the other side of town. I turned around between the signs identifying this addition as RidgeWood (the landscape was as flat as my hand and not a mature tree in sight) and started up the street in the opposite direction. The jewelry store had a new name on the sign and Laurel Bacon's dress shop was now The Vogue. The shoe store was gone, probably like Hastert's grocery and Bergdorf's bakery a victim of Wal-Mart. Bergdorf's restaurant building had survived under a glitzy new façade studded with neon beer signs. Hank Costello's greasy corner had been replaced by a sparkling BP station: six two-sided fuel pumps and a convenience store. The building that had been a pool room and beer joint and its adjoining vacant lots had been pre-empted by a handsome one-story brick and granite bank building, First National Bank of Columbia, complete with a drive-in portico, an ATM, a night depository, and shade trees that had to be at least 25 years old. The implement store of old was now two stores. The one devoted to hardware and seeds had familiar names on its signboard, Hawkins & McNabb. The other, Buzz's erstwhile bicycle and implement store, now displayed lawn mowers in the window. Its side yard was full of enormous green and yellow machines without which (I presumed) modern farmers could not function. The lawn mower store had a huge sign 20 some feet up in the air, lights blinking out PACE in letters three feet tall, in the daylight.

I turned around in the PACE drive and turned in at Elm Street to find Madam Anna's house. The house was gone; the outline of a fire-blackened foundation marked a filled-in basement where it had stood. Some of the huge old trees survived although there were fire scars on the trunks that faced the house place. A few flowering shrubs ran along the side fence that divided Madam Anna's lot from the Pace's back yard, but all the remaining area was grass, smoothly mowed and edged. A fire! And not recent! Was there a story here? I'd be looking up a surviving Pace to ask some questions. Now I drove on to the streets I had trudged carrying the *Radio Crier* on Friday afternoons, stuffing it into the bright yellow tubes of *The Columbian*. The Post Office remained in its old location, the car repair shop too, although renamed.

The proponents of asphalt paving had prevailed for a majority of the back streets. Each simple clapboard house of yore seemed to flaunt a satellite dish. I found all the churches where I had trolled for news and shared the fellowship spreads after the services. Wesley Chapel had fallen on hard times; its charming stained glass windows were partially boarded over and its flower beds, once glowing all summer long with marigolds, were weed-grown. The other churches seemed to be thriving and even expanding with parish hall additions. Parking areas that I remembered as gravel were now asphalted.

CHAPTER ELEVEN

By 10:30, I had made a fairly thorough tour of the old Prosperity. I saw no point in looking over the new housing. It was likely no different from thousands of commuter habitats around cities and towns all over the country. Every house would have an attached two-car garage, a family room, and cable hookup. What recommended housing here in Prosperity was its distance from a major urban center and its hinterland of unpolluted air and green fields—Indiana at its best. I turned back to pull up in front of Madam Anna's lot on Elm Street. I parked and got out to walk around. I found a log bench at the back of the lot and as I sat down on it, I wondered who had placed it there and who used it. Was it someone like me who knew Madam Anna and honored her memory with a few moments of restful silence in the twilights of early morning or late afternoon?

"Hey, who're you?" I heard a child's imperative voice.

Coming from the gate in the Pace's fence was a little girl, maybe four years old, dressed in a frilly pink dress. She marched straight up to me, stood still, and smoothed her frills with both hands.

"This is my new dress. I have to go to the doctor for my shots and Mommy let me dress up so I wouldn't cry when they hurt. Who're you?"

"I used to live in that house a long time ago." I pointed at its remnants.

"Nobody lived there since I came here. Was it nice? This yard is nice. I like to play here."

"Yes, it was very nice and the yard was even nicer then. What's your name? Mine is Katharine."

"Oh, oh, oh!" she squealed. "That's my name too, only Mommy and Daddy and the boys call me Kitty. Grampa's the only one calls me by my whole name."

"What's his name?" I hoped it was Harold, but her answer came quick and firm.

"His name's Grampa."

Just then a woman's voice called from the Pace's back porch. "Katharine Anne Pace, you get right back over here before you get that dress dirty!"

"That's what Mommy calls me when she means business! 'Bye."

And she danced off, flirting her skirts with every step, her blond mop flying in the breeze of her passage. I had noticed she had the same bright blue eyes that shone from Mariah Pace's rosy face; surely she was a grandchild, then I did a double take—more likely a *great*-grandchild. I found myself wondering if the PACE store was open now and whether I might find Harold there. I rose and leaving my car parked where it was walked over to PACE. I wondered too, if I did find Harold, whether he would recognize in this expensively turned out elderly female, limping a little with an arthritic knee, the bright-eyed, fresh-faced girl sitting across from him at Mariah Pace's bountiful table.

CHAPTER TWELVE

I entered the cool, dim cave of the PACE establishment and made my way though ranks of motorcycles, bicycles, lawn mowers, tillers, and edgers. Shelves on shelves were loaded with biking and lawn care accessories. A bell had jangled as I closed the door behind me and a diminutive woman in a scarlet jogging suit came toward me, asking if she might help me.

"I was hoping to speak to Mr. Pace."

"He's in the back. Harold!" she hollered.

A young man in chinos and a button-down shirt emerged from a back room.

"Can I help?"

"I hoped to speak to Harold Pace, but he would not be so young a man."

"Oh, that's Dad, he's out back working on a baler. I'll give him a call."

The young fellow whipped a cell phone out of his pocket and spoke briefly. Then turning to me, "He says come on back if you don't mind him with greasy hands. This concrete walk goes all the way, he's on the right side of it."

I went out through the yard full of looming yellow and green behemoths until I heard banging and looked off to the right to see a tall, lanky man, in a John Deere cap, bushy white mustache, bent over a machine. Tentatively, I said,

"Harold?"

The man straightened and his face lit up in undisguised pleasure.

"Miss Culhane!. How did you get here? What brings you to

Prosperity? Gosh, this is a happy surprise. I'd shake hands but if I did, you'd never get yours clean again."

"It's good to see you, Harold. You're looking well. It seems you have prospered; this is quite an establishment. And a fine son to help you run it."

"Turned the business over to him last year, semi-retired, that's me. Lots of changes in Prosperity but you don't seem to have changed much."

"Oh, but I have. I can't imagine how you could recognize me after all these years."

"Oh, Miss Culhane... I'm sorry, it's probably Mrs. by now and not Culhane any more.... But whatever it is, I'd know you anywhere. I had quite a crush on you and used to sit and stare at you when you weren't looking. Guess I memorized you."

"Well, it's still Miss Culhane but I expect you to call me Katharine. By the way I met your granddaughter this morning, all dressed up in pink to go for her shots. Quite a charmer. Say, can we get together for a long talk when you're not busy?. I didn't see a restaurant on Main Street but maybe Columbia...."

"Hey, my wife, Crystal, died a few years ago, and I been bachin' it since. I can whip up a pretty good meal, so why don't you come along to my house about six and we can eat and talk and catch up. Have you got time to visit Mom? She'd be tickled pink. You remember her book. She's got all the scoop on each of her lodgers in that book and she goes over and over it. There's names she lingers on, yours is one of them."

"I want very much to see her, if not today, soon. I'll be in Prosperity for several days. But maybe I could drop in this afternoon."

"She's in Sunset Manor Assisted Living in Columbia, fell

a while back, broke a hip, diabetic, needs insulin, but there's nothing wrong with her brains. Have young Harold sketch you out a map to the Manor—around here we call it the Home—in Columbia. Gosh, she'll be so pleased to see you."

"Thanks, I'll see you at six, where?"

"Do you remember Second Street? I got a little yellow house with lots of white gingerbread trim on the corner of Second and Oak. Young Harold and his family live in the old house."

"Say no more, I can find that easy, I delivered many a *Radio Crier* there in the old days."

Young Harold drew me a map and marked a good place in Columbia for lunch. He said Mariah would get back to her room from her lunch about 1:30. He warned me of the tight security at the Home—have to keep out scammers and people soliciting the old folks, better be prepared to present all your identity papers. I walked back to my car and left for Columbia. Having eaten, I passed by a florist and picked up a beautiful cyclamen to take to Mariah. I would stop by on my way back to Prosperity and buy cut flowers for Harold's dinner.

CHAPTER THIRTEEN

I had my driver's license ready when I signed in at the reception desk but the plump, white-haired woman there recognized me and waved it aside.

"I'm Bessie Carew. I used to know you and your name is still the same."

And I knew her: Bessie Carew, who used to let me read the notes she took at the village council meetings in Prosperity. Now she lived here at the Home and worked part time in reception. We chatted briefly, then she directed me down a long hall to Room 111. When I knocked, Mariah's voice came strong as ever,

"Come in! Come in! I'm so glad to see you. Harold called to tell me you would be along. Whatever in the world brings you to Prosperity again?"

She stood supported by her walker, no longer rotund, instead shrunken to the transparent skin and frail bones of old age; no longer rubicund, her face as white as her hair; but as much a personality as ever. She had me sit down and made me tell her all about my "doings" since I'd gone from Prosperity. She showed me her cherished "ledger of lodgers." She also told me something surprising. She and Frank had celebrated their fiftieth wedding anniversary a year before he died. It seems that after 20 years away, Frank had returned, begged her forgiveness, and they had started over. She had never divorced him or had him declared dead so it was all still legal, she said with a twinkle. Frank had taken the savings earned as a bookkeeper for the circus (after his tightrope walker had dumped him and until the circus folded) and turned them over to Harold to expand his business. Then he had gone to work for Harold, keeping the books for the business. Easy tears came to her eyes as she said,

"Before Frank died he tried to make up for them twenty years and we got to be a happy family again. I miss him more now than I did while he was away in the circus."

I noticed she was beginning to tire so I decided to go, promising that I would be back. I still had questions to ask about Madam Anna but first I'd see what Harold could tell me. There was plenty of time, I would be in no hurry to leave Prosperity.

Dinner with Harold was very pleasant. His small house was beautifully kept. He said his daughter-in-law, Laura, came over once a week to touch it up. And Harold had learned how to cook from his mother. I had forgotten how good Indiana pork, roasted and garnished with onion-perfumed dressing, was. Carrots and peas and homemade dinner rolls accompanied it and the dessert was lemon pie. We lingered over coffee, then adjourned to the living room where every surface was studded with photos of the youngest Paces—twin boys, John and Thomas, and Katharine.

"Oh," Harold said, leaning back in his easy chair, "my life has been very good. Crystal was a loving wife, Dad came back into the family, and now there are the young folks, handsome and healthy. And the business provides well for us all."

"Tell me, Harold, about Madam Anna. I wanted to ask Mariah but I hesitated to wear her out with what is probably a long story."

Harold began with a date, January 8, 1962. It was memorable. The Paces were awakened in the middle of the night by a very loud noise. They looked out to see a rush of flames rising from Madam Anna's house. It had first exploded, now was burning. Harold called the fire department but the station was in Columbia and it was 20 minutes before they could get there with their equipment. When they did arrive, the fire was well advanced and punctuated repeatedly by more but smaller explosions. The firemen refused to enter the burning house as long as explosions were occurring. By morning the fire had burned out and there were no more explosions. Then it was a job for the county coroner, the state fire marshal, and the sheriff. They had to wait until the ruins cooled enough to go in and look for a body. They located it on the burned out springs of the bed, charred, unrecognizable; the fire had been unusually hot. When the fire marshal learned of Madam Anna's business, he questioned Harold about her supply of fertilizer. Yes, she kept bags of it in the basement. No, it wasn't commercial stuff, it was some chemical. That was according to the 25-year old Harold, but later, in his business Harold became an expert on fertilizers, especially ammonium nitrate and its potential for explosion and flammability.

The fire marshal eventually inferred that ammonium nitrate fertilizer in the basement was the origin of the devastation. The coroner was a mortician and disclaimed any forensic skill in examining a body so badly burned, so the sheriff invoked a pathologist from the state laboratory. The sheriff later told the Paces there was no evidence of smoke inhalation which meant Madam Anna was dead before she burned. In their grief, there was at least relief that she was not burned alive. In the absence of evidence to the contrary, the verdict was accidental death, not homicide or suicide. The coroner registered a verdict of natural death for Madam Anna, perhaps from a stroke, and the fire marshal decided that the ammonium nitrate in the basement had ignited coincidentally from defective electrical wiring. Mariah Pace told them about Madam Anna's brace and her helplessness when she had removed it. The sheriff had found the metal stays and bands near the bed and the body. The scenario of her death developed thus: she, feeling ill, had undressed and gone to bed; the fertilizer happened to go off; she, shocked and surprised by the explosion, had suffered a mortal stroke or heart attack before the fire had reached her body. And there the matter rested.

Harold finished his story. "It was a sad, sad thing. I felt really bad about it, all the more since about a week after the death notice appeared in the paper, a lawyer from Columbia came looking for me. Madam Anna had made a will leaving her property to me because I mowed her lawn and did handyman jobs around the house. She had life and property insurance. I was named beneficiary for both. I used the money to buy into the implement store. So Madam Anna, from beyond the grave, started me off in life."

"Did you talk to her before it happened? Did she think she was threatened by someone or had she a presentiment of death?"

"Several months before, she asked me to check and update her door locks and latches, but she didn't seem very worried about 'em. Why?"

I decided to tell Harold about the trunk (but not about the contents) and the letter with the words "maybe something bad will happen to me" but he had no explanation or even speculation to offer. We talked a little longer generally about the changes that fifty years had brought to Prosperity. I learned Sol Baumer had developed Alzheimer's disease and his daughter had taken him off to an eldercare center near her home where he had died. Sally Frye was still about town, badly crippled with arthritis, but with a good word for every encounter. Oh, yes, as Harold said, changes, people and places, but not all of them bad. The building boom had given a second life to Prosperity, there was a doctor now and the Wal-Mart had a pharmacy. We made an early night of it and I was recording the day in my journal by ten o'clock.

CHAPTER FOURTEEN

Mariah had given me her phone number and specified those hours when she was available for a visit or a call. She was a very busy lady since she participated in every activity the Home offered: exercise sessions, lectures, movies, trips, you name it. When I called her at 10 A.M. the next day, she was resting from her exercise session and would welcome a visit after her hair appointment,

"Come about three, I'll treat you to tea and cookies in the social room."

The social room was a beautifully decorated salon, elegant furniture, soft music playing from hidden speakers, table spread with linen and an array of cookies. Fifteen or twenty residents and their guests were in attendance. A pleasant hum of conversation filled the room. Charming nooks invited private conversation. Bessie Carew presided over a handsome teapot and flowered cups and saucers. Mariah settled herself in a chair and beckoned me to another. A candy-striper placed a plate of cookies and a cup of tea for each of us on a small table between our chairs. I was dumbfounded by the amenities I was finding in what TV had conditioned me to expect as a contemporary snake pit for the elderly.

"Church ladies make us a project," Mariah said. "A respectable way of earning a better seat in heaven at Jesus's right hand. Some of 'em are just plain hypocrites. They'll end up in the back row anyway."

Nobody was going to pull the wool over Mariah's eyes. We chatted for a while before I broached a discussion of Madam

Anna's fate. Mariah's eyes filled with slow tears when I brought it up.

"We were friends for a long, long time. I was maybe the only friend, other than you, that Anna let into her life, and she didn't even let us in very far, did she? But it was an awful thing to happen to her. I'm not sure to this day that it was an accident, but I don't know what else it could have been."

"Did she confide any worries or presentiment of trouble to you in the weeks or months before it happened?"

"No, but she did seem to me to be organizing things for a kind of final event. For instance, she was giving her prize violets to church fund-raising affairs. She had Harold clear out her poinsettia stuff—the plastic that protected the floor, the tables that held the trays of pots, her stock of pots—she said she was going out of the plant business. She asked me over one afternoon for coffee and fresh-baked bread and sent me home with a pretty little vase that she said she had since she was a child; I was to take it as a memento of our friendship. When I broke up housekeeping, I gave the vase to Laura; she had it appraised and found out it was a rare and valuable antique. It was as if Anna was saying farewell gradually to all of us. I knew how old she was, and although I didn't think she was ailing, I just took for granted she was winding down. I understand that even more clearly now that I'm old and thinking about letting go of life."

"Did you know she had a trunk shipped to me? It would have been in the fall of 1961."

"Oh, yes, I remember, she had Harold take it to Federal Express in Columbia and ship it to your Washington address. More mementoes, I suppose."

I then told her about the "something bad" phrase in the letter I found in the trunk. It didn't seem to wake any further memories in Mariah's mind, so I dropped the subject. By 4:30, Mariah was ready to go back to her room to rest before her dinner. I bade her good-bye and promised another visit before long.

CHAPTER FIFTEEN

The next morning I picked up Harold before he started his day's work. After he had inspected and exclaimed over my Mercedes (every man I've ever known has been more enchanted by my ritzy cars than by me), he directed me to the cemetery in Columbia where Anna's remains had been laid. I had never had occasion to visit the place when I lived in Prosperity. The burned remains had been cremated again after the pathology examination and the sheriff had turned them over in a simple urn to Harold and Mariah. They had arranged to inter it in Mariah's parents' plot. A simple granite slab about one foot wide and two feet long bore Madam Anna's name and the date of her death; there had been no reliable record of her birth date. We had stopped on the way at a nursery and I bought a pot of *Rudbeckia,* thinking Madam Anna would have enjoyed their bright yellow blooms. Harold and I sat quietly for a few minutes on a nearby bench and then left for Prosperity, without much to say to one another.

After I dropped him off at PACE, I stopped in at Hawkins & McNabb. Walt Hawkins was behind the counter but I had to tell him who I was. He apologized for not recognizing me but explained he had cataracts in both eyes and was scheduled to have them operated for lens replacements. I asked about his family.

"Well, maybe you remember Sally McNabb. When we married we got started on our family right off. Ended up with five boys and two girls. My oldest boy went to medical school and practices in Columbia, two of the boys are career Army men, the youngest boys were twins, one of them is a lawyer, the other works in the bank. Lucy, my oldest girl, works here in the hardware store, likely never to marry, doesn't think any fella is good enough for her. Mary Lee, the younger one, is married and living in Washington State. I got twelve grandchildren and three great-grandchildren."

Whereupon he hauled out his billfold and showed me their pictures. When I commented on the name above his store, he said, "Yeah, Sally's daddy bought it about twenty years ago and coaxed me to quit at the cheese factory and work here. When he died, he left the business to me and Sally and we made it Hawkins & McNabb. We've done real good."

"Do you happen to remember Madam Anna Suvorov? The woman who had a plant business in the house behind the Paces. I've been hearing a pretty sad story of how she died. I lodged in her spare room, you know, when I lived in Prosperity."

No, he said, heard of her but didn't know her. His brother Clem did some carpenter work on her house once, said she had most of it converted to greenhouse plants. "Clem felt real bad when she died in that awful fire. Moped around for months afterwards. To this day, Clem is scared out of his skin by fire, even a little bonfire or a grass fire."

I found that interesting but didn't pursue it. I remembered Clem Hawkins as Walt's younger brother, and something of a ne'er-do-well. He and Johnny Card hung out together in Columbia at Pete's Bar in the old days. He must have straightened up and learned the carpenter's trade. I told Walt good-bye and left. As I went out the door, I met an old woman hobbling and bent over a cane. I was sure it was Sally Frye. And indeed it was. The hand she stretched out to me was badly deformed by arthritis. We stood for only a few minutes to chat, just long enough to plan to meet for a good long talk at the First Baptist ice cream social scheduled for Saturday afternoon. I was in no hurry to conclude our encounter but standing was obviously painful for her. I came away from our meeting thanking my lucky stars to have escaped from my arthritis with no more than a gimpy knee.

In the next few days I drove around the county, refreshing my memory of Columbia and the country roads around Prosperity. I dropped in on Mariah whenever she had a few moments to spare from her multifarious activities. Her current assignment was a committee to plan Fiesta Day. She predicted lots of heartburn after the Tex-Mex menu but thought colorful dress-up and paper sombreros, accompanied by Maalox, would mitigate that disadvantage. The ice cream social at the Baptist Church was a great success and Sally Frye and I sat talking a long while. She related how in 1963 Sol had begun to go without underclothing and then sit around with his fly unzipped, to the horror of the ladies who came to place ads for rummage sales. At length, Sally had called Sol's daughter in Florida to inform her of his behavior. The daughter came at once, got a judge to declare Sol *non compos*, put *The Crier*'s assets and business up for sale, and hustled Sol off to an old folks home near her. The daughter told Sally to take whatever she wanted from the premises before it was sold, and Sally took Sol's ancient Royal typewriter, just for old times sake. The building sat unused for a long while, although someone had come and carried off the files of back issues to the Columbia Historical Society. Then *The Crier* building was torn down and the empty lot converted to parking. Sally was living comfortably on her savings and Social Security and Medicare despite the painful arthritis that plagued her. She enjoyed the tales of my travels and writing and rather envied my chance to see far places but all in all, she said, Prosperity had treated her just fine and she had no complaints.

During my drives, I located the Tyler County Justice Center in Columbia. It was a modern building in attractively landscaped grounds, built recently enough that handicap accessibility had been designed into the structure rather than jerry-rigged to meet Federal requirements. I appreciated the elegant ramp as I entered the building. The receptionist directed me to the Records Office, where a smartly uniformed young woman grimaced in dismay when I asked to see a 38-year-old file.

"Those files are buried in the basement and I'm not sure the public is authorized to poke around in them."

She was going to find more reasons to deny my access, but I noticed a copy of one of my recent romance novels on her counter. Turning it to bring the cover photo and my real name into view, I asked for the file again.

"Land sakes! Are you her? I just love your books. I've read 'em all, I think. Would you sign this one? Please write my name above yours, it's Luetta Caine."

I was half ashamed to take advantage of her attachment to my trashy stuff but I did autograph the book, and she did get permission from her supervisor to pull the Suvorov file. It took her about half an hour to dig it out.

"Is this it? The tab says S-u-v-a-r-o-f, but the inside reads Suv-o-ro-v. Died in a fire in 1962. Well, OK, you can sit over there and read it. I can't let it go out of the office."

The file was bulky; it contained not only the reports of officers on the scene but also the reports of the coroner, state pathologist, and fire marshal. I read everything and made notes but the only new information I gained was the names of the sheriff and deputies who investigated the event and the pathologist's note that the well-preserved brain of the decedent showed no evidence of a stroke. I asked Luetta about the investigators—the sheriff died years ago, one of the deputies had retired to Florida, but another one, though retired, still lived in Columbia. He used to come in and chin with her boss. His name was Duke, she thought. I guessed that must be the deputy signing his report as John Wayne Tutwiler. I asked for a phone book and found an address for him. Thanking Luetta and promising to send her a signed copy of my next book as soon as it came off the press, I left to find Tutwiler.

CHAPTER SIXTEEN

John Wayne Tutwiler lived in a neat white clapboard cottage on a shady street on the outskirts of the town. A burnt wood sign on the gate sported the name. Another burnt wood sign beside the door displayed the house number. I suspected that a wood burning set figured large in someone's hobby equipment. The front door stood open behind the screen door, and when I knocked on it, I heard a full-throated shout from the depths of the house.

"Come on in! I been expectin' you. You're late."

"Mr. Tutwiler? My name is Katharine Culhane and...."

"Oh, Hell! I thought you was my house help. I ain't buyin' anything so if you're sellin' just turn around and leave."

A man in a wheelchair came whizzing out of a back room to face me in the front hall. He was a big man, burly, bald, red-faced, still wearing his pajamas although it was already ten o'clock. He looked surprised and interested when he realized I was female and well-dressed. I explained my presence and purpose briefly and he ordered me to follow him to the kitchen, where the remains of a breakfast of cold cereal and Pop-Tarts still lay on the table.

"Here, clear that stuff away and sit down. I ain't made coffee yet this morning or I'd offer you some. If Deely gets here pretty soon, I'll put her to it. Now what's this about the fire in Prosperity? Say, stop that Mr. Tutwiler business, call me Duke."

I explained my interest in Anna Suvorov's death and the reason for my ignorance of the circumstances until I returned to visit to old friends in Prosperity a week ago. I had to answer a lot of questions that Duke asked me about my life. Sitting in a wheelchair had to be boring, and he obviously thought I was more interesting than television. He approved of all my travels, told me he had slogged through French mud during the *WAR* (the *BIG* one). He also approved of my settling now in California, sunny and warm all the time; but he was disappointed that I didn't know any movie stars. Duke's home helper, Deely, tall and rawboned in a blue denim overall, finally arrived and made coffee, then insisted on doing his bath and getting him dressed before Meals-on-Wheels brought his lunch. She was brisk and businesslike and brooked no argument from the old man. She had other clients to attend to and tolerated no delay. Since I had all the time in the world and wanted Duke's full cooperation, I waited patiently until Deely turned him out freshly shaved and dressed. She departed, leaving an order for him to do up his dishes and wipe down the kitchen counters. Tough love therapy, I assumed.

I got him started with what I had heard and told him I wanted to hear what he knew. His memory of details of that long-ago event was extensive. It had been, after all, an unusual occurrence for a peaceful rural community. He told me little that was new to me, most of his story was covered in the formal report or repeated what Harold and Mariah had told me. That is, until he got to reminiscing about the weather and the crowd on that cold January night.

"Had a time keepin' folks back. They was all standin' there shivering in coats pulled on over their night clothes. Most of 'em was real mad the firemen wouldn't go in. Couldn't understand that stuff was still explodin' and roof beams fallin' down made it too dangerous. I remember Walt Hawkins and Mrs. Pace was making a lot of noise, and that photographer from *The Crier* was trying to push inside the tapes. I didn't live in Prosperity and I didn't know most of them neighbors that was makin' a fuss. But I had to take a couple in hand. The Card kid and Clem Hawkins kept pushin' and shovin' people to get in the front row. I had to threaten to arrest 'em. I knew them because they had a reputation in Columbia for disorderly conduct at Pete's Bar and when I was dealing with them that night, they smelled of drink and smoke. But by then we all smelled of smoke. All the same those two fellas seemed to think they had a right to get in and play firemen."

I was struck by an idea. "How was everybody dressed? You said coats over night clothes, but was anybody fully dressed?"

"Come to think of it, that photographer, and Johnny Card and Clem Hawkins was. Shoes 'n' all. Mrs. Pace was wearing slippers and a big old raincoat in the beginning but she went back to her house and dressed, put on heavy shoes and a big old woolly jacket. Came out again, totin' a big urn of hot coffee and had her boy bringing cups and a big platter of donuts for the firemen and deputies. She kept the coffee comin' until daylight, but she run out of donuts before. She was some lady. I often wondered what become of her."

I was pleased to inform him she was alive and well and living at Sunset Manor in Columbia. He chuckled and nodded,

"Runnin' it, I'll bet."

Meals-on-Wheels came just then and the elderly man who delivered it said it was the end of his route, so he sat down to keep Duke company while he ate. I left with Duke's invitation to return whenever I could, didn't need to have a reason, he just liked looking at a pretty woman. With flattery such as that, like of which I hadn't heard for a lot of years, I was sure to repeat my visit.

CHAPTER SEVENTEEN

The publisher of my romance novels had finally tracked me down, and I found galleys of my latest novel in the day's mail. I always let style and punctuation to the house editor, but as much as I despised the genre, I personally vetted galley meticulously for spelling and grammar. So I spent the afternoon carefully proofreading. That evening, bringing my journal up to date, I took stock of the facts I had on hand about Madam Anna's demise and made notes of those I had yet to find.

The scenario constructed at the time had satisfied the officials of the day that she had suffered a natural death and subsequently an accidental cremation. The more I learned, the less sure I was that their take on the facts was rock solid. What if someone had smothered her in her bed and then torched the house to cover up murder? Why would anyone enter her house and intentionally or unintentionally do her harm? My alternative scenario involved an intruder searching for valuables, waking her and hearing her call out, then pressing a pillow over her face to quiet her. She was old, frail, helpless without her metal brace, it wouldn't have taken much to kill her. And what better way to conceal unlawful entry and murder than with an all-consuming fire? Whoever had torched the house didn't even have to know about or utilize the fertilizer in order to get a big fire going.

I saw that I would have to pursue some definite lines of investigation and proceeded to list them.

➤ What had caused Madam Anna to think something bad might happen to her? Had someone she distrusted learned of her valuable icons? Had there been a newcomer to town or a stranger asking questions?

➤ I would question Mariah, Harold, and Sally Frye about that.

➤ Had newspapers reported her gifts to the church bazaars? Maybe with a picture that someone had recognized from days long gone and far away? The files of *The Crier* had been taken to the Columbia Historical Society; *The Columbian* must have files, too. I would start searching both *Crier* and *Columbian* back issues for 1961 and 1962.

➤ Then there was Clem Hawkins's "moping" after the event, and his and Johnny Card's presence, fully clothed and maybe drunk, at the event. I would ask Harold, Mariah, and Sally about them too.

A review of my list prescribed a schedule of activities for at least the ensuing week. I went to bed with a feeling of satisfaction that I had found some ways to further my information base. I cautioned myself against gloating—I knew a lot more than I had known but there was not yet a structure that hung together.

CHAPTER EIGHTEEN

I spent the next morning in the dungeons of the Columbia Historical Society. The Historical Society was located in an historic building, Tyler County's first Courthouse, a Gothic structure of red brick and local limestone. The first floor (where I tarried only briefly, promising myself a longer visit on another occasion) was an interesting mishmash of this and that. Prominently displayed were an officer's uniform from World War I in a vertical glass case (on loan from Mr. Carter Blass) next to a horizontal display of presidential campaign buttons (on loan from Mr. W.W. Wickham) next to a handsome china cabinet, its antique glass door cracked and repaired with transparent tape, filled with a collection of plates (on loan from Mrs. W.W. Wickham). I found it less a museum than a regional attic. A bicycle of the bone shaker vintage hung suspended from the dome in company with a scythe fitted with a cradle for hay harvesting. When I asked for the files of back issues of Prosperity's *Town* and *Radio Criers*, the attendant showed me to a door discreetly located behind a pillar and cautioned me to watch my step on the steep stair. She switched on a scatter of 25-watt bulbs dangling from the basement ceiling, pointed to a table in a far corner, and informed me I was on my own.

The air in the basement was at least as old as the building, stale, blessedly dry but so heavy that resident dust lay quiet even in the stir of my passing. A gooseneck lamp standing on a corner of the long table of newspaper files introduced a 100-watt spot of light into the gloom. *The Town Crier* had been bound in hard covers, but Sol had opted for tabloid size for *The Radio Crier* and those issues were shrouded year by year in heavy craft paper and tied with twine. Out of curiosity or maybe nostalgia or maybe unwarranted egotism, I opened a 1950 package and looked up stories with my by-line. Not bad, I decided. Thanks to my youthful energy and verve and Sol's clever editing, they stood up fairly well. I skimmed through issues from the years I had been on *The Crier* staff, noticed a few mentions of Johnny Card's escapades (one involving Clem Hawkins as well), but saw nothing that related to Madam Anna. I opened the 1961 package and began to read carefully. In the second week of May, I ran across a feature that, without naming Madam Anna, described her plant business and magnificent outdoor gardens in glowing terms. It had been written by a stringer from Columbia, printed in *The Columbian*, and cribbed for publication in *The Crier.* There were no photos but I made a note to hunt up the original article in *The Columbian*'s files. In a June issue, a three-line item mentioned a "visitor from hammer-and-sickle land" come to observe local agricultural methods, name of Victor Antonov. The next issue, another three lines announced Mr. Antonov's praise of Prosperity and its excellent agronomic practices, and foretold his departure for the wheat harvest in Nebraska. I was surprised that Sol had made so little of a foreign visitor, until I recalled his deep-seated and vociferous disapproval of all things Communist. I'm sure he decided to give no more than token coverage to one of "them," even when one of "them" spoke kindly of things U.S.A.

In the 1962 package the explosion, fire, and death of Madam Anna became occasion for an EXTRA, complete with pictures, headlines, and extensive quotes from officials and onlookers. There were ten copies of this EXTRA in the 1962 package and with only a minor twinge of conscience, I extracted one of them, folded it carefully, and tucked it in my handbag. I wanted to read it at leisure and look at the photos with a strong light. Making the occasional note, I read on in 1962 until there was no further mention of Madam Anna or the destruction of her home. Harold's inheritance got no space. I tied up the packages I had opened, relieved to be done with them and anxious to leave the dungeon, but also saddened by my look backward. I emerged from the basement, and writing a generous check to the Historical Society, I escaped to the fresh air and sunshine of a lovely summer day.

As I ate lunch in a lovely little tea room near *The Columbian*'s offices, the day turned dark, with towering black clouds and gusty winds—typical Indiana weather, bearing out the universal saw "If you don't like the weather, wait 10 minutes and see how you like it then." I was paying at the counter when the first raindrops fell but I made it to the newspaper's door before the heavens opened in earnest. I rather dreaded another session in a dim lit dungeon but was pleased to encounter a state of the art microfiche reader in a pleasant cubicle that made my search of old issues easy. I quickly found the original article about Madam Anna's horticulture that Sol had adapted to the *Radio Crier*'s readers and printed out a copy. I also found a rather long feature about Victor Antonov's agricultural tour. I printed a copy of that as well. I was amused to find that the *Columbian*'s account of the events of the night of January 8, 1962 was a barely disguised paraphrase of Sol's report, although the photos (credited quite properly to Sally Frye and *The Crier*) were different. Typical media practice: when you can't report from the scene, you quote whoever did. I printed a copy of that article and when I found Madam Anna's brief obituary, that too. Beyond these few items, *The Columbian* had little to offer on the subjects I was researching. The fire and death quickly became old news and faded from notice. I packed up my copies and was ready to leave by 3:15. I emerged from the newspaper building to find the sun shining brightly in the sky and reflecting blindingly from vast puddles in the streets, bits and pieces of limbs and leaves scattered hither and yon, and at least four shop signs blown from their moorings. I was a little concerned for my car which I had parked in the shade of giant oaks on a side street but no harm had come to it. On the way to The Nook, I stopped at a stationery store for a powerful magnifier. I also made a stop at a supermarket salad bar and assembled my dinner. My hostess at The Nook maintained a bottomless pot of coffee (shades of Mariah Pace) and I was well furnished for an evening of food, drink, and a lot of reading.

CHAPTER NINETEEN

I laid out my notes, clippings, and copies in chronological order and started to enter my findings on the computer. *The Columbian*'s articles on Madam Anna's gardens and Victor Antonov's American mission came first. *The Columbian*'s reporter had refrained from using Madam Anna's name (at her request, I was sure) but described her as a Russian-born émigré and a woman in her senior years. The article dwelt particularly on the variety and rarity of certain kinds of African violets in her stock; it noted that the grower, who was planning to retire from business, was offering them free of charge to church fund-raising bazaars. Interested groups might contact her at a P.O. box number in Prosperity. There were a couple of rather nondescript photographs of the grounds, although one of a pot of *Mandevillia* was a sharp close-up, beautiful even in black and white. A candid shot of Madam Anna bending over to pull a tall *Allium* into a more favorable position for the photographer showed her face in three-quarter profile. Anyone of her acquaintance would have known at once who the garden lady was. So much for anonymity.

The Victor Antonov story was headed by a very clear shot of him shaking hands with the county agent, a man named Baker Meiklejohn. The article described at length the nature of Antonov's mission. He was some big shot charged in the U.S.S.R. with restoring productivity in farmlands ravaged by the war and slow in recovering. He had a heavy, stolid face, thick brows and a massive forelock looming over a stocky, muscular body in a badly fitting suit. In the interview, he emphasized the agricultural similarities between the U.S. and his country and the benefits of exchanging agronomic know-how between the two countries. He was staying in the Hotel Mersman in Columbia and condescended to find it adequate. From long experience in interpreting the pronouncements of political hacks, I had the impression he was a Party man, mouthing Party slogans, nothing of a farmer, totally a bureaucrat, someone the Party could trust to travel abroad without a risk of defection or embarrassing revelations of the regime at home. He would travel on from Indiana to the Midwest wheat harvests, to join there with other members of the mission.

I was suddenly struck by the clustering of the dates and an emerging relationship among these articles. *The Columbian*'s garden lady feature with photos was published in the last week of May, the article and photo of the visiting Russian in the first week of June. Sol's crib of the garden article was published in mid-June, and his abbreviated items about the Russian visitor appeared in the next two issues of *The Crier.* It occurred to me that Baker Meiklejohn might be a useful contact, if he were still alive and if I could find him. He wasn't in the phone book. The next morning I stopped by the County Extension office in Columbia. Fortunately the agent was in.

"Do you know a man named Baker Meiklejohn?" I asked. "I understand he was once county agent here. I couldn't find a phone number for him and I'd like to talk to him about the visit of a Russian agronomist some 40 years ago."

"Oh, sure. Old Bake," he grinned and chuckled. "He's retired and living with his married daughter in Covington Cove in Prosperity. He's made a hobby of cutting lawns on his John

Deere riding mower. He'll be more than willing to talk; in fact, he'll talk a leg off you if you let him."

Armed with a hastily sketched map, I found Mr. Meiklejohn happily cruising a vast corner lawn, pleased to interrupt his round and to talk. I escaped with both legs intact and some more information. Mr. Meiklejohn's watery blue eyes snapped with remembered ire as he talked.

"Victor Antonov! arrogant bastard—excuse my French—I had orders from the Department to be at his beck and call for the better part of a week, chauffeur him around the county, put up with him. I never figured out what good his visit was going to do for the U.S. or for Russia. I drove him around, pulling off the road whenever he ordered so he could look at this field or that, which he did through the car window. He never even got out of the car, didn't know diddly squat about farming. The first day he came to the office, he got all het up about a clipping from *The Columbian* that we had on the bulletin board, something about a woman in Prosperity and her garden. He said he recognized her from her picture, used to know her. The address in the article was a P.O. box in Prosperity, so I had to drive him there. He either bribed or bullied someone in the P.O. to tell him where this lady lived. I stayed in the car while he made a false start, went up to this big white house on Main Street. He soon came out and said the place he wanted was around the corner. I stayed in the car while he knocked on the door, went in, and stayed about an hour. Came out real grumpy and I took him back to Columbia and dropped him at Pete's Bar; he spent all his evenings there swilling vodka and chewing the fat with some of the regulars. I had to take him back to his friend's house the next day but no one came to the door when he knocked. I was never in my life so glad to see the last of anyone as him looking out the bus window as it pulled out for some place out West."

I thanked Mr. Meiklejohn and escaped from a spate of anecdotes he was more than willing to share. So I now knew Antonov had been in Prosperity and had seen Madam Anna. I wondered whether his visit was the omen that made her think something bad might happen. Antonov's looks and mien by themselves seemed intimidating to me. That afternoon I was visiting Mariah and I asked her if she remembered the Russian asking for Madam Anna that afternoon so many years ago.

"I sure do," she said. "I was doing my baking and he busted in like he owned the place. Why I remember him so well—we had a cat, pretty little orange tabby, and that devil deliberately kicked him out of the way. He was mad because Madam Anna wasn't in my house and he had to leave and go around the corner to hers." Her indignation was still alive after all those years. "We was right fond of that cat; thank goodness, he wasn't hurt."

"Did Madam Anna ever say anything to you about his guy's visit? Mr. Meiklejohn said he was in her house for about an hour. She must have known him or at least tolerated him for some reason."

"No, she never mentioned it and I never asked. She was real close mouthed about her past. She probably told you more than me."

I dropped the subject but I surely did wonder what Antonov had to say to Madam Anna, especially since Antonov was grumpy afterwards. I still had said nothing to anyone in Prosperity about the icons in the steamer trunk. Before returning to Prosperity

I had taken them to the Getty Museum for authentication and appraisal. The curator who examined them was blown away. Priceless, he kept saying, especially the Saint Basil. From internal evidence, he was able to date the painting to Byzantium and the 13th century; the gold frame had been added in the 16th century, probably by a monk skilled as a goldsmith. Worth at least a million to a collector, he said, breathing hard. He was less enthusiastic about the other one. It dated pretty surely to the 17th century and was recognizable as a piece by a well-known Russian iconographic artist. The value lay chiefly in the gems that studded the frame; in the curator's opinion it would only bring three or four hundred thousand at auction, a mere pittance. Hearing what he had to say, I put the two icons on loan to the museum with the proviso that they would not be exhibited without my written permission. I was assured they would be kept in the highest security the museum could muster. But a question kept gnawing at my mind. Had Madam Anna told Victor Antonov of them, or had he guessed or known she had them? He had said he had known her; I wondered where, and when, and how.

CHAPTER TWENTY

That evening I turned to *The Crier*'s EXTRA on the explosions, fire, and death of Madam Anna. I read it very carefully but nothing new surfaced except the photos Sally Frye had taken of the crowd that night and of the ruins the following day. The reproduction of the crowd pictures was typical *Crier* quality— grainy and cropped to two-column width. I could barely make out individuals in the crowd and even less reliably identify them. I knew they were good pictures because Sally Frye had shot them. It was Sol's ham-handed treatment that ruined them for me. When I turned to *The Columbian,* the photos were a great deal better, still Sally's work, but a more competent compositor at work. I could identify Mariah, Harold, Walt Hawkins, Harry Bender, and Mr. Hastert but a great many of the faces were too small or too blurred. Even my new magnifier was no remedy. Then I used some common sense and decided to enlist Sally Frye in my study of the photos. I called her, apologizing for interrupting her evening TV viewing, and learned she had every negative for every picture she had ever taken for *The Radio Crier* as well as those she had sold to *The Columbian.*

"All filed by date in my coat closet. I'll be happy to show you what I've got. Come over tomorrow afternoon and we'll look 'em over. Don't fuss about interrupting my TV evening—it's an old Miss Marple mystery on PBS and I not only remember whodunit but how it was dun."

The next morning Sally showed me her file and had me pull the negatives for January 8, 1962 and several days thereafter. Her hands were not flexible enough to select or shuffle them but as I spread them out on her kitchen table, disappointment and discouragement reigned in my voice,

"I'll never be able to see anything on these."

"Of course not, you'll need prints and enlargements. Pick out some of them and I'll tell you the only photo lab I will allow to handle them"

"Will you allow me to use all of them? There's always an unexpected find to be expected. It's called serendipity, isn't it?"

She laughed and agreed. We sleeved all the negatives in envelopes and I took down her directions to the photo lab. It was in Indianapolis, just off the east leg of I-465.

"See George Karapoulis. He may be able to do them all in one day but if you have to stay over, there are nice motels in the neighborhood."

So the next morning, I packed an overnight bag and the carefully packaged negatives and drove off to Naptown, as I and my fellow students called it in my college days at Franklin. But of course, Indianapolis was now more megalopolis than sleepy Naptown. The pall of brown smog that used to hang over the city was gone and every thoroughfare hummed with frantic traffic, some six lanes wide. I found the Peerless Photo Shop without any trouble and George was very helpful; he thought the job would take a day and a half, why didn't I do some sightseeing to pass the time. So I parked the Mercedes at an upscale Marriott just down the street, registered, had a *haute cuisine* dinner in their elegant dining room, and slept like a baby in a freshly redecorated guestroom. I picked up brochures of local features worthy of a look, and chose the Indiana Historical Museum, the Eiteljorg Museum, and the Zoo, all in the same comfortably small zone downtown. With an eye to the vigorous traffic of the town, I took a cab to get there. Footsore but thoroughly entertained by a morning of museums, I started a sunburn with an afternoon at the Zoo: I loved the polar bears and penguins, cheered like a child at the dolphin show, took the train around the African veldt exhibit, considered an elephant ride but the line was too long. I realized my life had not included such simple enjoyment for a long time. I made up my mind to remove my nose more often from the grindstone of my writing career and use it to smell the roses.

George called the next day at noon and at 1:30 I picked up a fat packet of prints. I thanked him at some length. As he took my check, he sent me off with a word for Sally.

"Glad to help. Just say hello to Sally and tell her I miss the good stuff she used to send us. She's a real pro, I hope she's happy in her retirement."

The next morning, Sally welcomed back her precious negatives like lost or strayed offspring and had me refile them. Then we sat down to look at prints. They were numbered in correspondence to the numbered negatives which in turn represented a time sequence from Sally's arrival at the fire scene and so on to the end of the sets. The enlargements were very good, sharp and clear, and I could recognize most of the faces. Those I didn't, Sally could.

"Who are these two guys?" I said, pointing to one of the earliest pictures in the time sequence. "They're fully dressed, their pants legs look wet, and their faces are sort of dirty."

"The one in the mackinaw is the Card boy, the other one is Walt Hawkins's younger brother, Clem I think his name is."

"What do you think they were doing there?"

"Well, I heard one of 'em say they were passing by and saw the fire and ran to try to do something. Said they got a garden hose hooked up but then the house exploded and they had to back off. That deputy," she pointed to Duke, "had to settle them down, they were pretty hyper, did a lot of pushing and shoving to get to the front of the crowd, probably had been drinking. The pair of them had a reputation for that. Probably comin' home from a bar."

"But don't the bars close at 1:00? All the papers say the explosion occurred at 3:00 A.M. I wonder where they were between times."

"Maybe stocked up with beer in the car. I don't know of any place for after-hours drinking; the sheriff had just run a campaign to close those joints down. I remember because Sol was sort of fussed that the EXTRA took precedence over his plan to feature the sheriff's success in that week's issue."

The roster of onlookers generally changed as cold and boredom thinned their numbers. Some went home, put on more clothes, and came back; some just went home. Mariah and Harold showed up in a good many shots, hot coffee and donuts in hand. In the later part of the sequence Johnny Card and Clem Hawkins were less frequently to be seen and more deputies and firemen appeared. I bundled up my collection of prints and tried to pay Sally for their use but she was adamant in her refusals. As I left, I noticed her Lay-Z-Boy was pretty ragged and since I was sure she depended on the comfort it afforded her aching bones, I made a mental note to send her a gift card adequate to the purchase of a new one. I figured she wouldn't be able to refuse that. I carried the prints back to my desk at The Nook and arranged them for future review. I wasn't sure they had told me all there was to tell.

CHAPTER TWENTY ONE

As I shuffled the photo prints and notes, I let my mind wander. That was a trick I had learned when encountering a snag in the flow of words in one of my novels. Occasionally my mental roaming put me to sleep in my chair but not this time. Instead I became aware of the number of times "Pete's Bar" turned up in recent conversations. I knew where it was, on a back street on the south side of Columbia, and I recalled that it had come into being not long before I had landed in Prosperity for the first time. I had never patronized it, then or now, since it had the reputation of a dive catering to the blue collar crowd. Not that I looked down on the blue collared; my career had placed me on a stool or in a booth in many a working man's hangout, and I liked beer better than the hard stuff anyway. A stop at Pete's Bar definitely had to be on my agenda. But I would have to look to my wardrobe. The Chanel suit and Gucci accessories wouldn't do, even designer jeans would get a suspicious stare. So I went shopping at the Wal-Mart for sneakers and off-the-rack denim shirt and jeans. I was surprised at how smart I looked in the outfit; the only thing that might have clashed was the careful coif of silver hair and expert makeup. Looking in the mirror as I toned down the makeup, I had to laugh. How much distance had intervened between my old ways in the old days in Prosperity and my current condition! In 1952, I would have thrown on this inexpensive new outfit, slapped on fresh lipstick, and been out the door without a second look.

I parked the Mercedes a couple blocks away from Pete's Bar, stuffed my wallet in the back pocket of my jeans, and locked the Gucci bag in the trunk. I hoped I was prepared for a call at a joint of dubious fame. The front was paneled solid in dark batten board; a single sweep of neon said "Pete's;" the only window was an 8-inch square in the door. I entered the interior gloom rather tentatively; I had chosen 2 P.M. for my visit, expecting to avoid the late lunch drinkers and the early after-work clientele. I needed the barkeep to be relatively free if I hoped to learn anything from him. I took a stool at the end of the bar, ordered a beer, and opened the conversation with trivialities about the weather. Then,

"What do you hear of Johnny Card and Clem Hawkins these days? Last I heard they hung out here a lot. I used to know them when we were young and carefree."

A lie in pursuit of truth is no lie—dubious ethics but a well-worn reporter's axiom. The bartender was a guy in his fifties, clearly too young to answer questions about the old days. Pushing the mug of beer at me and swiping the wet off the surface of the bar, he surprised me with a useful answer.

"Well, Clem got religion a few years ago and drinkin' ain't allowed. So he stopped comin' in. Johnny's back since he's been out of jail but only hangs out between spells in AA. He got scared when the docs told him his liver was shot and he was tryin' to quit but he's sorta backslid."

"Gee, what got him in jail? When I knew him, he was kinda wild but nothin' serious."

"Grand theft auto, I heard. He don't talk about it."

I decided to ask about previous bartenders, told this guy I was a freelance reporter and hoped to sell a story about Pete's as a landmark business.

"Ask Pete, he can give you the whole story. That's him

sitting at the table in the corner. He's here every day, making a mug of draft last for hours, takes several refills but he makes it last."

I looked at the man at the corner table. He was old, really old. A few white hairs straggled over the bald spot on his head, his bony face was a mask of wrinkles, his fleshless hands were clasped over the curved handle of a white cane. The mug had been recently replenished.

"Would he be willing to talk to me?" I asked.

"More than willing. He sold the business ten years ago when his eyes went bad but he couldn't get out of the habit of coming in. The new owner makes him welcome and all the free beer he can drink."

I walked over to Pete's table and introduced myself as M.J. Cuthbert, free lancer, hoping to write a story about the Bar. I thought a bit of discreet anonymity was called for in case Johnny or Clem heard someone was asking questions about them. I hoped Pete's tippling didn't seriously affect his mind or memory, and my hopes were rewarded. He was talkative, lucid, and coherent. He told me he had come home from WW II with savings enough to put a down payment on a bar and in 1947, this was it. He scrabbled for years to pay off the mortgage but he bragged that he had always kept the place clean enough for the city inspectors. He was proud of his clientele, an orderly bunch, although the ball bat he kept behind the counter had something to do with that. It was easy to ask him about old customers. The Russian had been a rare occurrence and Pete could relate to the drop how much vodka Antonov had consumed and how he rambled on.

"What did he talk about?" I asked.

"Depended on how much vodka he had put away. Early in the bottle it was how much better life was in Russia than in Columbia—grand buildings, glorious history, smarter politicians, blessings of Communism. He bragged a lot how the government in Russia looked after everyone, no one too poor to have medical care or decent housing. When the level in the vodka bottle was a little lower, he moaned and carried on how the war killed so many Russians, his brother among them, and ruined so many plans for progress, including those for more productive agriculture and more modern housing. By the time the level was almost at the bottom, he was ranting about Russian treasures, immensely valuable golden pictures from splendid churches, stolen by traitors to Mother Russia, and smuggled out of the country. He'd screw up his face in a wink and say 'Some of those stolen treasures even come to a stinking little place called Pros-Pros-Pros-terity.' Then he would mutter about 'that old White Russian woman, big thief' and pass out. He was some piece of work."

"Did anybody besides you listen to him?"

"Yeah, whoever was sitting at the bar. He sat right there on the end with his back to the wall, as if he thought somebody was going to stab him in the back. Made me wonder what kind of place he drank in when he was home."

"Did Johnny Card and Clem Hawkins ever hear him talking about treasures and an old Russian woman?"

"Don't see how they could not have. Neither of them had a job at the time and they was comin' in spending their unemployment compensation on beer every night. But they didn't pay no more attention to the Russian than anyone else did. They spent most of their time on the stools at the bar, jawin' with buddies. Come to think of it, they sat at the bar for years although sometimes they had jobs and didn't come every night."

I let Pete go on with endless anecdotes, fifty-three years in the bar made for lots of them, and telling his stories stoked the fires of life in his ancient body. Finally, I said I had to go, thanked him for an entertaining afternoon, and promised him a copy of the article I planned to write. And I meant to deliver on that promise. In fact, I wrote the article that very evening, signed it M.J. Cuthbert, and mailed it to *The Columbian* the next day. I guess I hadn't lost my touch; the article turned up in *The Columbian* three days later (obviously it had landed on the editor's desk on a slow news day). I clipped it and mailed it to Pete. I hoped he would like it; I had written it from a kind heart. M.J. Cuthbert, freelancer, would get a check for $25 at her Malibu address.

CHAPTER TWENTY TWO

The next time I sat down to bring my notes up to date, I reviewed a summary of my information on Johnny Card and Clem Hawkins.

- ➤ Johnny and Clem were ne'er do wells, and they knew an old Russian woman lived in Prosperity. Clem had even done some carpenter work for her.

- ➤ They had had every opportunity to hear Antonov raving about Prosperity and an old Russian woman and stolen treasures there.

- ➤ Being jobless and short of money was a usual condition for both of them. Were they above breaking and entering to go after valuable stuff to sell?

- ➤ The photos put Johnny and Clem at the scene of the fire and their wet and dirty appearance told against them. Where had they been between one P.M. when the bar closed and three P.M. when the fire drew the attention of the town?

- ➤ If treasures had been a motive for hitting on Madam Anna's house, why did it take months, from June to the following January, for them to try it? Were they in jail, or working out of town, or just scared off by Madam Anna's new locks and latches?

> ➤ Their lives after the fire were in no way run of the
> mill—Clem had moped for months after the fire,
> later he got religion. Johnny ended up in jail for a
> major felony.

I wasn't ready to charge them with the fire. After all, it had been months after Antonov's stay in Columbia that the fire occurred, but I seemed to see a pattern. I judged it was time to pin down more details with a focus on the pair.

Before I tackled the men separately and in person, I wanted to talk over my data and my inferences with Mariah and Harold. If I was off-base, Mariah especially would be quick to spot my error. And Harold, of course, was in the midst of Prosperity's daily life for the past 50 years and would have insights that I, as a stranger, would have missed. So I called up Harold and asked him if he would set up dinner for us and Mariah at his house. If he would let me, I'd have the dinner catered. When I proposed it, however, and told him the reason for our get-together, he insisted on preparing and serving dinner himself, providing I went after Mariah and brought a fancy dessert to finish off the meal. No problem. So at 4:30 the next afternoon, I was helping Mariah out of the Mercedes and up the front walk with one hand and balancing a Boston cream pie with the other. Harold came out and got Mariah and her walker through the door and settled in the living room for *hors d'oeuvres* and tomato juice.

We saved the serious talk for after dinner entertainment. Dinner was wonderful: fried chicken, mashed potatoes and milk gravy, sweet potatoes, peas, and carrot coins (no salad, Harold didn't hold with rabbit food). The dessert was good, but rather disappointing despite its reputation as the finest product of the best bakery in Columbia. We had our coffee in the living room and Mariah and Harold listened carefully when I pulled out an *aide memoire* I had prepared and read off my current conclusions and guesses. A long silence followed my final point. Then Mariah spoke up,

"I always wondered what spoiled Clem Hawkins's life. Walt told you he 'moped' after the fire and indeed, he must have. But he did it in a psych ward at the state mental health facility— that's what they call it now, but then it was just a detention center for crazies. Walt put him there because he had fits and kept tryin' to commit suicide. People didn't talk about it, they felt so sorry for the Hawkinses. But then some new medication come into use and Clem did pretty good on it. When they let him out, Walt got him a job with a framing crew and rode herd on him for several years. Then Clem got a hillbilly girl in trouble and her family made him marry her, and she took over looking after him. She lost that baby and they never had any more and it was a good thing, Clem barely made enough to support him and Cleo. She worked for me for a couple months when I had a busted ankle and needed help with the cleanin'. She was the religious one and she made him go to church and prayer meetin' twice a week. He went on Social Security and Medicare as soon as he qualified, and him and Cleo are livin' in a trailer over on the west side. Walt and Sally help out, I'm sure. I wouldn't be surprised if his mental problem wasn't guilt; them Hawkinses had more than one relative with shaky head pieces. Whew, I think I need another cup a coffee to wet my whistle after tellin' you all that."

We poured her another cup of coffee and then it was Harold's turn. He had been in the front row of onlookers at the fire and he noticed particularly how messed up Johnny's and Clem's clothes were. One sleeve of Clem's coat was burned off and he was whimpering with pain until one of the firemen applied First Aid to his scorched arm. Maybe that's why Clem was so terrified of fire ever after. Both Johnny and Clem were wet and sooty but if they had got close enough to the fire to try putting it out, that was easy to explain. Harold hadn't heard much about them and their doings until he saw them at the fire. As for Johnny, he bummed around Columbia and Prosperity for years, supported by his father until Will died, then by his sister and her husband. They weren't very willing but he was family and even two jail terms couldn't change that. The first time he got sent up was for a bar fight in Indianapolis where he had gone looking for work. In the fight, Johnny hit a guy, knocked him into the rail at the bar, and the guy died of a brain hemorrhage. That was manslaughter, and he would have been out in four years with good behavior but he got in too many fights inside and ended up with ten more years. Once released, he got a job driving truck for a local delivery company and for a while it looked as if he had straightened up but he still drank every chance he got. Then a few years ago, he took off in somebody else's fancy car, drove it all the way to Mexico using a stolen credit card, got caught at the border, and it was back to jail.

"He's been out again now for a year or so. Looks terrible, like a sick man. He's livin' in a shed out on his sister's farm, drives a junk car into Columbia. They say he signed up with AA but he still goes to Pete's Bar every chance he gets. The bar in Prosperity won't serve him anymore."

I drew some deep breaths. If those two guys were

responsible for Madam Anna's death, maybe the ruin of their lives afterward was a consequence. I chose this moment to tell Mariah and Harold about the icons. They were not particularly impressed with their appraised worth, but they saw immediately their significance as valuable possessions of a helpless old woman living alone.

"I hate to say it," Harold said slowly, "because it isn't very Christian to think ill of anyone, but I think those two could have put their heads together in a plan to take advantage of Madam Anna. Maybe they didn't intend to kill her or to blow up her house but...."

His voice trailed off and Mariah took up the thread,

"Well, it may not be Christian to think it," she snapped, "but it would be downright unchristian not to do something! What are you going to do, Katharine?"

I looked at my good friends and the conviction and concern on their faces. They thought I had a case against the men. But I didn't know what I could do. Go to the law and ask them to open a cold case and be laughed at? The case had been closed years ago and there was no physical evidence of any of my surmises. Confront each of the two old men and badger them into confessing to a 38-year-old crime? And if I got confessions, what would I do with them? I just couldn't decide what I'd do. Finally, I answered Mariah's question.

"I don't know. I'll have to think about it. But I'm grateful that the two of you find it reasonable to consider there's something to my ideas so far."

We broke up our meeting then and I took Mariah back to Sunset Manor. We didn't talk on the way, but she pulled my face down to kiss it when we parted.

CHAPTER TWENTY THREE

The next morning, I rose to greet a beautiful day, my brain still in a muddle. What was I going to do? For the moment I put the problem aside, ate The Nook's breakfast of quiche and fresh fruit, then dressed in my sneakers and freshly-laundered Wal-Mart outfit. I got in my car and drove around more or less aimlessly until I passed the Columbia supermarket. An idea struck me and I went in, bought two over-priced bottles of spring water, a banana, an apple, and a cellophaned package of cheese and crackers. Then I went, now with a purpose, to the Pipsissewa State Park, parked the car in the empty lot, and with my lunch in its plastic bag slung over my shoulder, set out on the trails. For the first half mile my quandary went on the back burner while I got used to uneven ground in soft-soled footgear but once I learned to look down and choose my footing, my mind was free to return to the question: what was I going to do?

It was a week day and I seemed to be the only visitor to the park. I walked the deserted trails, turning aside on every cross trail and choosing every fork. I even took the bridle path to the stables, at this hour populated only by grooms. Tired, I sat down on a bench in a pretty little clearing and watched the wood around me. The trees were full of birds, flashy ones like cardinals and blue jays, drab little finches and wrens, and one very noisy woodpecker pounding away on a rotten limb. Squirrels bustled up and down, a possum came along snuffling in the leaf litter, a rabbit nibbled on a patch of fresh young grass. I had been a city denizen for so long that I found it remarkable how fearless these wild things were, but concluded it was because I was motionless on my bench. When I started to unwrap my lunch fixin's, some of the wild things grew more wary but others grew more bold. Cheese and crackers tasted like sawdust to me but a squirrel found them a delicacy and scampered away with both cheeks stuffed full. I drank deep from my bottle of water, then put the banana skin and apple core into a covered trash basket to the obvious disappointment of the blue jay. I began to walk again, slowly, still musing, organizing my thoughts.

I had built a whole scenario out of guesswork and a few facts. The scenario went something like this: Victor Antonov's loose talk at Pete's Bar had clued Johnny and Clem into "treasures" in the Russian woman's house. Whether or not Antonov had seen or merely suspected Madam Anna's valuables was immaterial. His ramblings could easily be interpreted or assumed to indicate that there were valuables of some kind or another in her house. Johnny and Clem knew of the old Russian woman in Prosperity, that she was Russian was common knowledge, Clem had done carpenter work for her. Antonov's visit had alarmed Madam Anna enough to ask Harold to update her locks and latches. She must have been troubled enough to think about a way to safeguard the icons and to decide to send them to me with a note that hinted at her apprehension. I guessed that her years had begun to weigh on her and she was shedding responsibility for her possessions. If she feared robbery or violence, the circumstances of her life had conditioned her to fatalistic acceptance of whatever the next days or months or years held for her personally. She would not have gone to the police with her suspicions. Not only did she distrust authority and its minions, she probably had no more faith in her suspicions than I had when I returned to Prosperity.

I couldn't explain the lapse of time between Antonov's bar talk and the fire and explosion at Madam Anna's house. Maybe, either Johnny or Clem had been in jail or out of town or both were working and flush with money. I was pretty sure that it took both of them to work up to major mischief, and that when they needed money they thought of robbery as an option. That the two of them had closed Pete's Bar the night of January 8 at 1:00 A.M. was believable, as well as the possibility that they had driven to Prosperity from Columbia, and emboldened by drink, entered and ransacked Madam Anna's house, and set a fire by 3:00 A.M. Their behavior before the firemen and police took over, Clem's severe burn, the way they faded from the scene as the number of investigators multiplied—those were suspicious facts. Could it have been that they had rummaged the house, waked Madam Anna—in bed and helpless without her brace, her phone in the kitchen out of reach, calling out in her alarm—and in panic, one of them grabbed a pillow and pressed it over her face to stifle her cries? Maybe there was no intention to kill, but considering her age and frailty, it would have been easy for a husky young man to smother the life out of her. Then, more panic, signs of a fruitless robbery and a dead woman to conceal—matches thrown here and there, catching curtains and dried out old wood, flames gushing— neighbors erupting from their houses, spotting intruders on Madam Anna's premises. Once at risk of being suspected of arson, the robbers, now murderers, pretended frantic efforts to quench the fire but were driven back by the first explosion of the fertilizer in the basement.

I could imagine the skepticism on the sheriff's face were I to relate that story to him. If he were kind, he wouldn't laugh but he certainly would point out all the weak points in my argument. Suddenly, I knew what I was going to do. I turned purposefully and following the rustic signs that directed hikers to the parking lot, I trudged back to the car. Back in town, I stopped to ask Harold the way to Johnny Card's sister's farm and Clem Hawkins's trailer home. He sketched maps to the farm and the trailer park but said I should ask at the trailer park office for Clem's unit. My intentions were perfectly obvious to him but he refrained from comment. However, as I was leaving the store, he called after me, "Take care!" in a meaningful tone.

CHAPTER TWENTY FOUR

The manager at the trailer park office did a double take as he looked past me at the Mercedes parked outside.

"Lady, this is no place for people with fancy cars like that...."

He must have thought I was a drug lord looking for a place to crash. I explained I was not looking for a rental. Would he kindly tell me which unit the Clem Hawkins family had and where it was located in the park. He could and did.

I drove down a back lane between rows of dilapidated mobile homes, savoring the irony that most of them had not moved in the last 30 years. I found Number 20 in the last row, a sagging tin box propped on concrete blocks, decrepit, paint peeling, but the concrete pad in front of it neatly swept and sporting an old wash tub full of marigolds in lusty bloom. The windows sparkled and the door step was scrubbed down almost to white wood. At my knock the door was opened by a lanky woman with a haggard, worn-out face. Her incongruously rich, dark hair, barely touched with gray, rippled in shining waves almost to her waist in the back.

"We ain't buyin' anythin' so you can move along."

"I was hoping to speak with Mr. Clem Hawkins."

"You must be from the Welfare. Oh, well, come on in. He's takin' a nap. Have a seat."

She flicked her hand at one of two captain's chairs pulled up at a scarred round table that stood between a living area featuring a threadbare sofa, a beat-up Lay-Z-Boy, and a 27-inch TV set and the counter of a galley kitchen. A card table set up next to the sofa was piled with newsletters emanating from a popular TV evangelist; several versions of the Bible lay open, the top one at Revelations. The whole place was scrupulously clean, although the surface of the linoleum on the floor was worn down to the backing in places. Mrs. Hawkins (Cleo, Mariah called her) disappeared down a hall leading to a bedroom and I heard her calling to her husband. A few minutes later, Clem came stumbling out from the back. The young man in Sally's photos had been tall, muscular, with regular and rather pleasing features surmounted by a heavy crop of dark hair. This old man was skin and bones, bald, bent, peering at me with red-rimmed, watery eyes. He sat down in the chair opposite me while Cleo took up a protective stance on a kitchen stool on his left.

"Mr. Hawkins," I said. "You don't know me although I know your brother Walt. I came to ask you a very important question. I know you were in Anna Suvorov's house on the night of January 8, 1962. What did you do there?"

I was shocked when the man reacted to my brutal words as if he had been struck by a bullet. He bent forward, wrapping his arms tightly around his skinny chest, as if to hold himself together, rocking back and forth in his chair. His face, already pale, turned ashy white and his breath came in gasps.

"Wha... wha... what?" he stammered. "The fire, the fire, it was awful, awful...."

Cleo interrupted, "He dreams of fire, nightmares, terrible nightmares all about fire. Why are you doing this to him? You're not from the Welfare."

"What did you do in Anna Suvorov's house that night? I want an answer. Tell me, it's important. Johnny Card was there too, wasn't he?"

Tears started to flow from his eyes and he launched into an incoherent spate of words. It was the breaking of a dam.

"Johnny did it... I was upstairs... We couldn't find anything... The Russian said there was treasures but we couldn't find anything but a few dollars in the kitchen drawer. Nothin' upstairs... Nothin' in the basement... Then Johnny says the old lady croaked, she was gonna yell... I was too scared to go in the room but I saw her on the bed with a pillow over her face... Johnny did it... I was upstairs...."

"Then what?" I was merciless and yet on another level I was full of pity for this terrified old man.

"Then what?" I hit him again with my question.

"Johnny said we gotta do something... A fire, a fire will do it... He pushed me ahead of him to the basement stairs... He grabbed some newspapers and wadded them up... Lit 'em with a match and threw the fire down the stairs... Made another wad, shoved it in my hand and lit it, and made me put it up against the curtain... Fire all around... Before long there was fire all around, in the bedroom, in the plant rooms... We got out the back door and Johnny threw burning paper up into that big old dry vine over the porch... Fire all around...."

"How did you get in the house?"

"When she had me to repair the floor in the plant room, she said if I'm not here, the key's up here above the back door. She still had that key up there. We was on the back porch... the house was flamin' and the vine was flamin'... I stumbled over somethin' and fell down and then there was this great blast and Johnny was pullin' me out on the grass. There was people startin' to come because of the fire and Johnny made me pull out the garden hose and we pretended we was puttttin' it out and then a piece of wood all afire flew at me and burned my arm...."

He pulled up his left shirt sleeve, disclosing a broad, shiny scar the length of his forearm. Cleo patted his shoulder and pulled his sleeve down, as if to relieve him of the sight.

"Nightmares," she said softly. "That's why he has nightmares. The fire has been burnin' him all these years in his sleep. God has been punishin' him with fire in the night. I didn't know why until now."

Clem broke down into uncontrollable sobs. Cleo stood behind him, patting his shoulder, her face a mask of pain and worry.

"What are you goin' to do about it?" she said in a small voice. "1962. That was almost 40 years ago, he's been payin' with nightmares the whole time we been married. I never knew why till now, but he said things in his sleep and I knew it was bad, whatever it was. What are you goin' to do now?"

A great wave of compassion flowed over me. Had Clem expiated Madam Anna's death by all the mental agony he had suffered in the years since his youthful crime? I didn't know. I didn't know what more I would do about Clem, but I did know I would confront Johnny too before I called my inquiry done. I got up and walked out. Cleo followed me as far as the door and stood looking after me with tragedy on her face as I drove away.

CHAPTER TWENTY FIVE

I drove over to the little park on Prosperity's back street and parked in a shady spot. I sat for half an hour quietly fingering Harold's map to the Cards' farm. I was shaken to the core by the havoc I had wrought by my questions to Clem; and not just his devastation, Cleo's too. Clearly she loved him, had shared a long marriage and a hard life with him, his collapse was hers as well. I wasn't sure confronting Johnny Card was the thing to do. He too was old, and I had heard he was sick. What damage would my questions do to him and his family? Who was I to play God? Or to descend like Nemesis? Finally, after many second thoughts, I decided Madam Anna's memory deserved the truth, all of it. And since Johnny had the rest of it, I had to confront him. With fresh resolve, I started the car and started out to Johnny's sister's farm.

The old Card farm was out in the country about three miles from Prosperity. The mailbox now said Munster and was situated at the end of a long lane that ended in a fine grove of trees. A white ranch-style house and a farmyard with a large red barn and several white- or red- painted outbuildings stood off to one side of the grove. I drove into the farmyard and stopped the car. An air conditioner unit protruded from the side of one of the outbuildings and I remembered that someone had said Johnny Card lived in a shed. A window box beneath a four-paned window in the door of the air conditioned building was stuffed with bright-colored plastic flowers. I rather dreaded bringing his sister into the picture by asking for him at the main house so I opted for knocking on the door above the plastic bouquet.

I had to knock twice before a face loomed in the window, and the door was opened a crack.

"Whaddya want?"

"Are you John Card?" I asked.

"Yeah, so...?"

"I want to talk to you."

"What about? I ain't got time to listen to no long spiel for insurance or vinyl siding."

"I want you to talk to me! I have questions to ask."

A spark of interest lighted his dull gaze and he stepped back to open the door and let me in. Maybe a visitor was a welcome break in his solitude. The space inside was rather nicely furnished, although the furniture was a vintage clearly discarded from the main house. A TV set on mute stood on a rolling cart in front of a recliner chair. There were apparently two rooms in the shed, a living room in the front with a hot plate on a built-in counter in one corner, the back room a bedroom. Through the door I glimpsed cheap cotton print curtains at the back windows and a pile of dirty clothes at the foot of an unmade bed but otherwise the house was clean and uncluttered. I suspected that his sister took a hand in keeping his house.

When I looked at Johnny, he did indeed look like a sick man, probably incapable of his own housekeeping. He too had been a sturdy looking fellow in Sally's photos and Harold had told me he was red-haired. Now his still bountiful hair was an odd red-and-gray mixture that looked even more odd above a pasty yellow complexion. A missing front tooth added to his appearance of general decrepitude. A hugely pot-bellied torso testified to a failing or failed liver; stick-like arms and legs poked out of a short-sleeved T-shirt and ragged denim shorts.

"Wait a minit. I got beans hottin' up for my lunch."

He went over and turned off the hot plate and entering the bedroom, brought out a straight chair which he placed for me before disposing himself in the recliner.

"My sister gives me breakfast and supper but I'm on my own at noon. Excuse my chair here but I ain't well and I'm more comfortable half layin' down. Now, what was it you wanted?"

"I know you and Clem Hawkins were in Anna Suvorov's house the night of January 8, 1962. What were you doing there?"

For a moment I doubted that the same kind of bold attack I had launched at Clem would work. I soon realized that I had not prepared myself adequately for the sly evasions and barely disguised truculence to be expected of a seasoned convict. A more gradual approach would perhaps have disarmed the habit of wariness of an old lag. In fact, Johnny didn't even flinch although his eyes grew sharp and shrewd. I could sense him deciding to brazen out his responses to me.

"Who are you? What right you got comin' here with questions about me and Clem?"

"My name is Katharine Culhane and I've just come from a long conversation with Clem Hawkins. I was a friend of Anna Suvorov, the woman who died that night and who burned up when her house was torched."

"What did Clem tell you? Whatever it was, you can't depend on it. He's a bonna fidey crazy."

"I thought he was telling the truth. Are you going to tell the truth?"

"Well, Hell, I might as well. That date was more'n 38 years ago. Clem and me was pretty well lickered up that night and Clem thinks he knows where there's somethin' we can turn into money. We was both pretty tapped out and the chance to get money was too good to pass up. Clem says that Russian in the bar a while back was tellin' how that old woman in Prosperity has got valuables and he knows where's a key to get in so we decides to look into it."

"Why did you wait so long to look up the valuables the Russian talked about?"

"We was doin' pretty well that summer, Clem was workin' and I had a girl on the string that just couldn't do enough for me, in bed or out." His leer was a weak parody of what it must have been when he was young and handsome. "Didn't need money then."

"Clem said you went through the house. Was the Russian right? Did you find anything?"

"Hell, no. She didn't even hardly have groceries in the cupboards. Did Clem say he found anything? If he did, he didn't share with me."

"A few dollars in a kitchen drawer. Where all did you look for valuables in the house?"

Johnny started to pick his words more carefully. He was building a story as he spoke.

"Well, we looked upstairs. Some people stash money and jewelry in the bathroom, thinkin' no one will find it under a floorboard or in a box of Kleenex in a cupboard. But wasn't nothin' up there. Then there was all them rooms on the first floor, smelled like mold and damp, long tables, some of 'em had plants on 'em."

"You must have turned on every light in the house, to be so thorough."

"Sure, we did. That house was so surrounded with trees and bushes, no one was gonna notice lights on, even in the middle of the night."

He fell silent, unwilling to admit either of them had entered the downstairs bedroom. But I pushed.

"You found the old woman in the downstairs bedroom, didn't you?"

"Well, where else would she be? She got sort of excited but she couldn't get out of bed, sick or crippled maybe; anyway, when I went over to her, she kind of squawked and fell back on her pillow. I figured she had a heart attack and was dead. Clem got all bent out of shape and said we had to make sure so he put the pillow over her face."

"That's not the way he tells it."

Johnny's face screwed up in an ugly grimace. "Course not, he's not gonna admit to snuffing her, or to setting the fires afterward. Clem was looking after Clem, then and now when he's tellin' it."

"Why is it I believe him and not you?"

As I spoke, I rose, picked up a pillow from the sofa, and stood over Johnny lying almost supine in his chair. Panic bloomed in his eyes; he was thinking *this crazy broad is gonna smother me.* Then he regained his confidence and gambled that the broad wasn't crazy enough to try it. His story changed a bit.

"Maybe Clem thought it was me but I know it was him. And he was the guy wanted to burn the place down. We never counted on that stuff in the basement exploding. It sure made a hell of a noise and got a bigger fire going than we figured. The old lady was dead when the fire started. I know that. Hey, what have you got in this? What was that old lady to you?"

"She was my friend," I said quietly and put the pillow back on the sofa. "I know who killed her and how you and Clem Hawkins ransacked her house and set it afire. If the law talks to Clem, they'll believe him, not you."

"Won't make no difference who they believe. I'm dyin', the docs that drained my belly last week say I only got another few months. If I have to go to jail agin, it ain't such a bad place to die in. I got more friends there than I got outside."

There was a kind of hopeless sadness in his voice. Clem had lived in a hell of guilt while Johnny was drinking his life away; both had self-destructed, each in his own way. Maybe Madam Anna's death wasn't responsible for the ruin of their lives, maybe some other unconnected event would have been responsible. Whatever, both had been destined for a miserable life and death. Clem was more fortunate than Johnny, his confession had perhaps purged his soul and he had Cleo to stand by him. Johnny denied the truth of his deeds and would die unrepentant and probably unlamented.

I turned and went out the door without a backward look.

EPILOGUE

I went to tell Mariah what had transpired, She was sitting in her wheelchair when I entered. I crossed the room with faltering steps, broke down into exhausted tears, fell on my knees in front of her chair, and wept into her lap. She patted my head and put her Kleenex box within reach. I finally controlled my emotion enough to tell her what confronting Clem and Johnny had disclosed. When I had grown calm again, she said,

"You did what you had to do. You found the truth. If you don't do anything more, it will be OK. The police won't want to do more. After 38 years, one man broken in mind, another broken in body, what more can the law accomplish? Madam Anna wasn't looking for vengeance and I don't think you were either. Let it be. Go back to your life in California and once in a while, think of me and Harold and Sally and all the good folks in Prosperity."

And that's what I did.